PRISON CITY

Book 2
Icecapades

JAMIE FARRELL

SR
Stillwater
River

First Stillwater River Publications Edition

ISBN-10: 1-950339-09-2
ISBN-13: 978-1-950339-09-9

1 2 3 4 5 6 7 8 9 10
Written by Jamie Farrell
Published by Stillwater River Publications, Pawtucket, RI, USA.

DEDICATION

To Joe, who not only helped me with the editing process, but helped me make this book even better.

To my friends and family who keep supporting me and are the ones that pushed me the most to get a second book in the series out.

BOOK 2
ICECAPADES

CHAPTER 1

Sheamus and I have had a lot of criminal encounters. We've seen more powers than we can even remember. Our job is dangerous and full of surprises but we would never give it up just to be "normal". When we wake up we aren't sure how it will all go about. Anything can happen and anything will happen.

Our confrontation with Christie and talk with Darkheart were three days ago. When we took on the simple mission to figure out what Andre Simmons was up to and who he was meeting, we never would have guessed that The Collector would be involved. Then I wouldn't have guessed that I would get into such a long fight with Mister Metal and that Darkheart would end it. Then we never saw that Christie had a whole plan of betrayal against Metal all figured out and that Sheamus and I would have to stop her from executing it. Plus we never would have expected a chat with Darkheart at the end of it all.

The point of all this is that sometimes as much as you plan out your day, it can all change in the blink of an eye. Sometimes you never see the unpredictable coming and sometimes the most predictable of things never happen. You can't guess how something will go from start to finish. Life is all about different paths you take and the choices you make along the way. Sometimes the best way to go about your day is to not stress about what is going to happen and just deal with it as it comes your way. Life certainly has a way of surprising all of us at the end of the day.

CHAPTER 2

"**S**heamus, you know how much I hate art and a mission in a museum isn't my idea of a fun time." I say. I am standing outside of Sheamus's bedroom and he is sitting at his desk looking through a file about one of the soon to be, ex-gang members of our fair city.

His bedroom is kind of like mine except it is a bit bigger since he has a bunch of filing cabinets that contain files on members and activities of Prison City. Other than a bed, desk, cabinets, dresser and closet his bedroom is nothing special. We don't need fancy furniture to be happy with where we live.

"Come on, Devon. We were asked to do this personally. Plus it will be nice to see the museum that Scotty has been working on for a year," Sheamus responds sounding like he is close to begging me. While he wouldn't beg me, I know his curiosity can be a reason why he wants to do so much.

"I really hate you." Scotty Braun is the well-known artist of Prison City. He apparently came in around four years ago after attacking multiple artists when he got jealous of their amazing sales and he was barely making money off his art work. He went from a local art gallery in the city to showcase solely what he could do and upgraded the idea to opening a museum that showcases the artistic talent of the prisoners.

Sheamus gets off of his chair and starts walking out of his room. "Well we might as well go to the meeting now." That stops me in my tracks.

"Wait now? You mean we get no preparation for this?" I am shocked usually we at least talked about what we could encounter before confronting a client. What the potential job was going to be, who else we could encounter, the level of danger and or risk we were getting into. So much has to be talked about.

"Well he wants to see us as soon as possible and I knew it would take a while to convince you to go so we might as well get it over with now before you change your mind." I am amazed that there was a whole plan to convince me. We are at the front door and he is basically ready to step outside.

"Excuse me just hang on a second," He turns towards me in mid turn of the doorknob. "We are going to this meeting, which is probably just going to be about a disgruntled elderly person who didn't get enough money for their painting seeing how it's in a museum. To me that seems like a waste of time when we could be looking towards something more." While I never mind the little missions I don't think it is significant to go to a dusty three story building that just showcases people's emotions in charcoal, ink, or pencil.

Sheamus laughs at me as expected. While normally I am not stubborn I can be stubborn on certain issues and then I become real whiney. "Let's go." He opened the door and left the apartment.

"Douche!" I yelled walking after him.

* * *

"You know this has always been a nice place to go." We have only been walking for twenty minutes but the scenery has changed drastically. Instead of a city-like atmosphere, we are surrounded by trees and heading up a hill. It is probably one of the nicest and peaceful places around. I sometimes come up here to get away from everything we have to do even if it is for only a half hour. But lately I haven't come up here much. Especially since part of it is private property.

"Grater's Hill I feel has always been one of those places that was off limits in terms of territory. After Grater died, not a soul has wanted to desecrate his space. I am just happy it is a place I don't have to look at constantly," he says looking slightly sad. A lot of people feel bad about the memory of Grater.

Grater's Hill used to be the headquarters of a guy named Grater who was a major head of a gang there some years ago. A little bit after Sheamus showed up in the city, there was a major plan with one of the gangs to blow up a huge populated section of the city to gain control of it. Grater, knowing the plan would happen soon enough, went off on his own to stop it. Getting to the part of the city that was going to be blown up, he warned people to leave as quickly as possible. But some people just weren't fast enough, so he used his powers to save them.

He was able to create shields and barriers around things and people using a type of psychic sense of impending danger. And in the last moments of his life that is what he did.

Using an extraordinary amount of power, he was able to detect when the explosions were detonating to a millisecond of it happening. He formed an extraordinarily strong barrier around the explosion, effectively containing it. He saved the city from five large explosions.

It had cost him his life.

The amount of power, energy and strength he used basically ripped his body apart inside of him and he died ten minutes after saving the city. Because of his sacrifice to the city it made a lot of people realize what life could be like here and so his whole gang went from a life of crime to helping out the city in different ways. One of those ways became making this hill anti-territory in a sense that no gang could claim it for their own and that promise lasted for years.

That was until about half a year ago when Scotty Braun decided to use part of the hill as his land for his house and museum. The only reason people allowed it to be used was because the artwork on display was from occupants of Prison City. Still today people have grumbled about it. The museum is partly a success though since apparently people enjoy looking at the creations that someone can make.

"It was annoying when coming up here never felt peaceful anymore. The construction of the building was noisy. Then after it was completed people kept coming back and forth. Honestly his memory is disgraced by it not being peaceful anymore," I say irritated. I have always enjoyed this place. One of the few reasons I am not a fan of this museum.

"Well just hope it won't be a hard job. Either way we are here." I look up and notice we were on the edge of the trees and have come out to a nice exposed view on a hill.

The one thing you notice here is the expansive view of the huge wall that separates Prison City from the rest of the world. But once you are familiar to living here you barely even notice it anymore and what you really see is the true view of the city. You can see all the important buildings and if you look hard enough you could see people walking around. Then I turn around to see the museum.

The museum surprises me more every time I see it since even though I am not into art or architecture it is a nice building to look at. It is actually quite beautiful. It reminds me of a type of old Greek building since it is made of white stone. It is also massive with three floors and quite long in length. On the side of the building is a sizeable pond that looks like it is cared for.

We are standing on the walkway to the entrance of the building.

"We might as well get this over with now. I'll probably end up regretting coming here after we are done with this meeting. More than likely it will be nothing," I sigh and walk towards the doorway.

"Douche," he says at me. I smile knowing I really am difficult.

CHAPTER 3

Opening up the main entrance door we are pleasantly greeted with one of the plainest looking lobbies you could have. The walls are painted a weird lime green color and a couple of small pictures are in the room, but other than that and the entry desk there is nothing else here. There are two doors in this room, one on the far end of the left wall and another on the right. In the middle there is a desk. The one on the right wall was ajar slightly.

"I guess no one is here," I say, moving to turn around until I hear a large bang and footsteps. The ajar door opens even more and a head pokes out.

"Sheamus and Devon, I am so glad you answered my call," a man speaks. The man is Scotty Braun. He is in his mid to late 50's with a sparse amount of grey hair and a thick bushy mustache. He is quite overweight and the top of his head comes up to my nose. He is wearing a full range grey business suit. He makes me feel underdressed since I am only wearing a blue t-shirt and shorts. Sheamus is just in a grey undershirt with shorts. When it comes to looking a certain part we really don't care.

"Well this morning when I got your note you said it was urgent, so we wanted to know as soon as possible what was going on," Sheamus responds immediately, going into information mode. Like usual, I let him do the talking since he gets more out of problem solving than I do.

"Follow me and I will tell you what is going on." He starts walking to the other door and we follow him through it. The room we enter is so much larger than the room we were just in. This room is painted white and has a lot more paintings. It even has a couple of sculptures in it. There are six other doors, two on each wall face that we can see, and a staircase that I assume goes to other rooms. "The point of this museum is to showcase the creativity of the members of Prison City through art. Sometimes making money in this place isn't easy, and that is where the museum can come into play. If you make an extraordinary piece you can bring it here and we will put it up for sale for you. The museum gets fifty percent commission, with the other fifty percent going directly to the creator." He states while walking through the room.

Leaning over to Sheamus I whisper, "For knowledge in case I want to punch this guy in the face, what exactly are his powers?"

"Basically he can manipulate ink. One of the biggest reasons he became an artist. Plus this museum is like a cannon for him against people," he whispers back.

"Each main room area like the one we are in," Scotty keeps talking without even noticing we are talking about him, "is basically my artwork only. Each of these rooms connects to more, each one dictating a different type of style. There are three different floors each with the same basic style. In each room the majority of artwork is made by the donations of people with a few other pieces made by me just to fit the style." We make it to the other end of the room by the time he finishes and he walks through the left most door.

The new room is also painted in white and has even more paintings than the last. There are dozens of paintings on the walls. They don't seem to have a theme amongst them and so this room probably solely focuses on paintings. They each have a little plaque next to them which says the name of the painting, who painted it and, if it is for sale, the price. Looking at some of the prices, I am not even willing to spend money just to hang something on a wall and look at it for the rest of my life. While Sheamus and I were looking around, Scotty gravitates towards the far end of the room and stands in front of a painting. It is four feet wide and two feet high. We move towards him to see what is so special about it.

"Meet my pride and joy. The Frozen Abyss. It was my first work I completed when I was sent here and I never had the heart to give it away. That is why I need you two here, I need you to guard it. I think someone might want to steal it," He says, yet getting more frantic by the end. But I am still confused.

"What makes you think someone would want this painting as opposed to the hundreds of other pieces of art here?" I ask. It makes sense. Why is he special?

"Because the threats are directed at me," he states.

"Wait, there are threats against you?" Sheamus asks. He seems shocked so apparently this tidbit of info was left out.

"Well of course otherwise there would be no legitimate reason to bring you here," he reaches into his jacket and pulls out two pieces of paper and hands them to Sheamus. "One of them came about three days ago and the other arrived yesterday."

Sheamus opens up one "Your most prized possession will soon be mine," he reads out loud. He folds the note and opens up the other one "Enjoy your time with your precious art before it's gone." He folds that one up as well. He passes them to me and I read them as well. They are on plain white paper and the letters are standard cut out letters from magazines and newspapers. The person wants to remain anonymous. Well now I understand the concern. But I still have a problem.

"You are certain that that painting is your most prized possession? Are you sure there isn't anything else in this gallery that this person might want?"

Scotty shakes his head in such a way I am afraid he could lose it "This is the painting I talk about the most and when I show people the museum I always show this one off. I am one hundred percent sure if they are stealing a painting it is this one."

"Scotty! Another one has arrived." A woman comes running through the door and practically shoves a piece of paper in Scotty's face. He grabs it, opens it up and reads it. Shuddering, he hands it over to Sheamus who reads it.

"Tonight is the night." He folds it up. "Same style as the other ones." He looks at me and I know why. This choice is up to me.

"Fine, we will figure out who did this."

CHAPTER 4

"**W**ho would want a painting? I don't know anyone in this place that just wants to take some guy's painting." I say as we return to the apartment again. "I think this is more against him and not about the museum or the painting itself."

"The notes would indicate that," Sheamus states, closing the door behind him and sitting down on the couch. I stand next to him, looking down at him.

"So who has it in for the guy?" I ask the obvious question knowing that we might be able to stop this before it starts.

"Do you really have to ask?" he gives me that "Are you kidding me?" look.

"You think maybe it's someone from Grater's old gang wanting revenge?"

"It is the most obvious answer I can think of," he says. I sit down next to him. It doesn't make sense to me.

"But if it's about him taking back Grater's land you would think they would be targeting the museum instead of just one painting."

"I said it was the most obvious I never said it made sense." He gets up off the couch and heads down the hall. "I want to go and check up on a few of Gater's former gang members. Want to come?" He asks like I really have a choice.

"I might as well. It would be nice to finish this before it even starts."

He pokes his head around the corner and smiles at me "Aww such a good boy even if you do whine." He moves his head out of the way before the pillow I throw at him makes contact.

* * *

Half an hour later we have a list of eight members of Gater's former gang that are either still in Prison City or are still alive in here. We are heading towards the first name on the list, Pearlene Elliot. Pearlene, or Pearl for short, is able to use the plant life around her to create a suit. Her file states that the EXO suit made her powers to control plants increase ten-fold. Without it she is barely able to throw a stick correctly. With it she can use every stick in a one mile radius as a needle aiming right at you.

"So do we know if she's hostile?" I ask. I don't feel like getting into a fight with an overgrown bush.

"All reports state for the eight members that they have gone onto better things in Prison City. So far none are in any gangs. But that might also be because they have such strict loyalties to Grater. We should figure out what they are doing with their life and what they are doing tonight. Anyone that doesn't have plans for tonight we might want to look into more," he explains to me and then stops. I stop along with him and understand why. We stopped at the local community garden, for those that used gardening as a form of relaxation.

The community garden is on a plot of land that has been cleared out solely for the use of garden plots. There seems to be about ten plots that are closed off and that people are using for their own gardening means. At the far end is a small shack that looks like it is inhabited but poorly cared for.

"After you," I say to Sheamus. We walk up a single path that leads from the road to the shack and leads past the individual gardens. We make it to the shack that has two big bags of dirt and a couple of gardening tools propped up against it. Sheamus knocks on the unstable door which opens barely a second after he removes his hand.

"Pearlene?" I ask.

"Yes. How can I help you?" Pearlene is roughly a few inches over five feet with long red hair that is down to her back with a couple of twigs stuck in there. In her early to mid-thirties, she is wearing a pair of ripped up jeans and a flannel shirt that looks two sizes too big for her. Her brown eyes look heavy like she just woke up. She looks to be covered in dirt. If I didn't know any better it looks like she just woke up in a forest instead of a shack.

"We are looking into a matter concerning Scotty Braun's museum. Someone is sending threats to him, considering the museum is on your former boss's land we were wondering if you knew anything about it." I figure getting right to the point could help us. Pearl though doesn't react much, if at all. I am not sure if it is because she doesn't care or is exhausted.

"Didn't even know it was happening. I've been quite busy with the gardens. Taking care of everything if someone doesn't care much about their plants," she pulls the door close as she walks past us. "Plus I moved on. I haven't left this lot in a month. There is so much to get done." She looks really tired and it almost seems like she can't stop talking.

"Ummm are you ok?" Sheamus asks immediately, putting his hands near his pockets ready for anything. I am also ready.

Pearl starts to shake her head "The plants they won't shut up. They talk to me all night. They alert me to all types of dangers. I have to keep helping them. They hate it when people abandon them so I need to stay with them. But they are telling me something now," Sheamus and I look at each other with him raising his eyebrow. "They are telling me," she gives us a hard look, "you are bad people." Suddenly from out of nowhere a tiny stick flew out from behind us and sort of attached to her chest and stayed there.

I flung from behind me a shadow whip that was wrapped around a shovel propped against the shack. With a mighty swing I slammed the metal part on Pearl's head. Instantly she fell to the ground unconscious.

"I was not expecting that," Sheamus states, moving over to her and checking her out. "She is fine and will more than likely be out for a few hours at least, and even then she won't be in any mood to rob a museum."

"So you think she could actually hear plants talking to her?" I ask slightly joking.

"Who knows," he says shaking his head. "Anything is possible. She does have powers over plants, but we can't worry about that now. Next name on the list."

* * *

Three hours later and six more names crossed off our list we have absolutely no leads to who could have problems with Scotty. One has plans for the night and the other five have already moved on with their lives and have no reason to go through with revenge. The last name on our list is Douglas Campbell. Probably the one person I wasn't looking forward to seeing in any type of situation. He was one of the few "weirdos" in the prison. By weirdo I mean even those completely powerful and dangerous don't go near him. People don't talk to him for fear of getting on his bad side.

Douglas is a power mimicker. He is able to mimic people's powers but only if he keeps in contact with them for a lengthy period of time. The powers he obtains slowly overtime grow weaker and he has to either do the process over again or lose them. While it takes months for him to lose powers and only a couple of hours to obtain, our records of his complete number of powers can't be known. Rough estimates put them in the high teens to low twenties. He is dangerous because the more powers you have the wider range of techniques you can do and thus can easily be able to fight an opponent no matter how tough they are. That is why we are going in and finding out if he has any reason to attack Scotty or the museum.

We arrive at a one story ranch style house that is completely dark inside except for a bit of light seemingly moving from room to room. It is made creepier by the fact that in a couple of hours it would be nighttime and the atmosphere seems to be presenting a creepy setting. Sheamus and I look at each other and slowly walk up to the front door. I knock on the door and after thirty seconds it opens to a dark haired man with a bushy beard. The door is only open up enough to see his head and an arm which held a fireball. This is Douglas.

"Can I help you?" he asks. The way he looks is creepy enough and makes me want to leave. No, I want to run.

"You used to be a part of Grater's gang, it seems that someone is threatening the museum that is on the land and we are wondering if it may be someone connected to Grater's gang from before." Being here is giving me the creeps. Even Sheamus isn't talking so you know this isn't a comfortable location.

"Well I've moved on to bigger and better things and don't have time for revenge." He starts licking his lips and looks at us harder than before.

"So we would like to know if you are doing anything tonight?" Now I am uncomfortable. I don't like him with the way he looks at me like he is going to eat me.

"Well if you must know I have a project in my basement. A guy that has the ability to produce no sound whatsoever. Now that's an ability I need for myself. So that will take a few hours and then I'll be out of commission till the morning at least." Well that crosses him off our list.

"Thank you for your time now we best be off," we turn around. "Good bye." We don't even notice we are running off until a few minutes later when we are completely out of breath. "So what is the plan now? We have no one else who could do this."

"I have no idea." Sheamus said who looks fearful. But whether it is due to us having no leads or what we went through I wasn't sure.

CHAPTER 5

A few hours later we are at the front door of the museum. We went home after seeing Douglas to recoup and get ready for our night here. It is now nighttime and even though we will probably be confronting a cat burglar tonight it seems oddly peaceful just looking over the city. We walk up to the front door and Sheamus pulls out an extra key and unlocks it. I walk into the front area while Sheamus locks the door behind us.

"OK, so what should we do?" Sheamus asks as we go toward the main gallery areas. The rooms have dim lighting on, enough so that you can see a bit but not enough for it to be using a ton of electricity. This helps us since no one would see that we are in a particular room when we guard the place.

"I honestly do not believe that one painting is what someone will be going after in this whole museum. I think we should check out the other rooms as well," Sheamus is nodding his head in agreement at me. "Plus someone could easily fly through a window, teleport in or just phase through a wall. It might be good to have all points covered," I explain even though he probably thought of it all as well.

"Should we split up?" he asks. I look at him horrified.

"Have you not seen any horror movies? We are in a dimly lit place with threats of someone coming here tonight to rob the place and do who knows what else. I don't care if we have superpowers, I don't want to walk around here alone," I explain.

Sheamus chuckles at that. "OK, OK. Let's go around through these rooms and see what we are dealing with." We start walking throughout the rooms on the first floor. We skip over the room we have already been in just to get a sense of what else we could be dealing with. The first room has the same color scheme as the one we have already been in but instead has paintings, sculptures and even a couple of a rough sketches for designs. Looking at the name on some of the works indicates that the room only has works created by a Corie Lamon. Never heard of her and so she must not be a troublemaker. We decide to move on from there.

The third and last room that branches off from the first floor main room seems to be an assortment of just random works by random artists. We don't see much more that could be suspicious. As we go along we are checking windows and seeing if anything could be hidden.

"Well if anyone put anything in here to spy on the museum I don't see anything," I say after looking behind a large sculpture of George Washington.

"Nothing here," Sheamus says after looking on a wall, "shall we try the next floor?" he asks already moving onward. We leave the room and start up the stairs.

"I don't think we are going to find anything. If I was going to steal something I wouldn't announce when I would be there. I certainly wouldn't announce that I plan on taking something. If anything this just seems like a prank."

Sheamus rubs his chin a bit. "Maybe that is the point of it all. Announce you are robbing the place.

The owner brings in people to protect the place. Then you come in to rob it," he puts air quotes around rob, "but the main point is to destroy the business. I mean what better way to destroy something than to allow super-powered people to battle it out. Something is bound to go wrong and do some damage." That is a farfetched idea but if it is true this could all just be a trap.

"Do you even believe that?" I ask. It is really out there and the only people I can see doing that would be someone from Grater's gang and we already checked them out.

He shakes his head. "No, but also I don't want to admit that we could be part of a trap."

We arrive on the second floor. Just like the first main floor this main floor only has works made by Scotty, most for sale but some are off limits for buying. We take the same precautions like we did with the other rooms, looking for anything out of the ordinary. We are once again disappointed.

"Are we seriously going to do this for all the rooms?" I am getting tired of looking at the same stuff and getting the same results.

"Trust me I am starting to get tired as well. I know how you feel now. This floor feels like the same as the first floor. I mean I would rather not have to be here all night." That is something I don't want to think about either. But suddenly I hear a loud bang and the sound of splintering wood from downstairs. Knowing this is what we have been waiting for we sprint downstairs. I instantly realize it feels cooler. Sheamus is one step ahead of me.

"They went into the painting room." We immediately follow but stop once we get to part of the wooden door. Half of it is still attached to its hinges while the other half was forced into the room. We hide behind part of the door and look in. Within a second I am filled with dread on who we see inside. Sheamus looks at me smirking "I see your girlfriend has been sending the threats."

Damnit! As if this night couldn't get any worse now I have to deal with Freeza.

CHAPTER 6

Two years ago.

Protein's Palace. It is a strange name for a restaurant but in terms of what they serve it is right on the money. Protein's Palace is the place to go if you want meat or eggs. For me, I am here for a date. I've been working for Sheamus for roughly three weeks and something he wants me to do is to try and live as normally as I can. So he's trying to hook me up on a blind date. While I thank him for trying to bring me on the straight and narrow and do something fulfilling with my time in here, I am unsure that dating a criminal is correct.

I am on the edge of downtown where there are more homes than businesses but Protein's Palace stands out more than usual businesses. It looks extremely elegant and I am afraid that the fifty dollars Sheamus gave me might not be enough for this date. It is a one floor building that is painted white. The front of the building has wide windows that display the inside showing waiters walking around and people eating their meals. At the entrance a man stands with a clipboard. Apparently this restaurant is reservation only. I walk up to a man who is probably one of the many bouncers employed around here.

"I have a reservation for two. It's under Sheamus." The man looks at his clipboard and nods. Not getting anything out of him I walk into the restaurant right into an entry room that holds a podium with a young lady behind it. I announce my reservation with her as well and she leads me to a small room towards the back of the restaurant.

In this room there are eight tables that are all for two people only. Of the eight, only six are in use. The decorations of the room are quite elegant and calming. Red wallpaper is on every wall with decorations hanging from the walls. Vases of flowers are in every corner of the room. Shockingly, there are no windows in any of the walls so this room must be intended more for privacy. Soft music can be heard throughout the room and I can tell this room is probably for couples only. The lady brings me to a table that is next to a table being shared by a large, built man and a tiny woman with her hair dyed a teal color. I try not to stare at the odd combination they share as a couple.

I sit at one of the chairs offered to me. "When your date arrives the waiter will come by to take your order but for now here is your menu." She sets one large menu in front of me and one across from me. With that she leaves the room. I look at the menu and realize the fifty dollars I was given would be more than enough considering none of the items on the menu, which were all burgers, steaks, or other kinds of meats, cost more than seventeen dollars. It only takes me a few seconds to decide on the gourmet cheeseburger, which is a cheeseburger but filled with tomatoes, lettuce, onions, and has a steak sauce added. It sounds amazing.

After deciding on what I want I look at the other people who are all talking to their partners or eating their meals. Even though I have been here for a few weeks I still have to remember that everyone here is a criminal. Plus I have to remember that they all have powers. Sheamus has told me to enhance my observational skills as they will help if I ever get in a confrontation. I decide to try it out on the couple next to my table. I look at them without being intrusive so I can figure out a bit just from what I can see. The large man is eating quite a big steak. Even though he is wearing a black suit you can tell his muscles have muscles considering the fabric is straining just a bit. I conclude that his power has to be strength based.

The woman is a different story. She is probably a third of the size of the man and is eating an ordinary burger that doesn't look special. She is wearing a fancy, red, and sleeveless dress that looks quite expensive. What is special about her is definitely her hair. I'm not sure why she would have her hair dyed to that color. It stands out so much and in this type of environment I don't think you would want to draw attention to yourself. Considering I can't see anything special about her that would say anything about her powers I wonder if her hair could have something to do with it. Maybe she has to dye it to get her powers or something strange like that.

"You must be Devon," a voice calls to me from nearby. I look up to the other side of the table and see a woman looking at me with a piercingly beautiful smile. She is around my age. She is thin and a little shorter than I am. Her eyes are a piercing blue while her hair is a combination of blue and silver and quite long. She is wearing a dress that matches her eye color quite well. I feel strangely underdressed wearing only a black button down shirt and jeans. In all definitions of the word she is beautiful.

"Yes and you must be Adelina Lupo." I stand up and pull out her chair while she sits down. I then go back over to my side of the table.

"Please, call me Freeza. It's what all my friends call me." I don't understand the meaning of the name since it doesn't match her real one, but I'm not going to be rude and not call her what she wants.

"Well, Freeza, it's a pleasure." At this point our waiter comes over and takes our orders. Freeza ends up ordering a steak which she has heard was one of their best items.

After the waiter left we decide to talk about ourselves. What our likes and dislikes are. What we think about the world at this moment. Even a bit of talk about our current place of residence. Sheamus has done his research on her and told me more about her than she has told me about herself. She is part of the famed Lupo family who owns businesses in forty-six of the fifty states and even in four countries outside of the United States. She was arrested when she got bored and robbed a store, ran from police and kidnapped a friend so that she would be hidden away. Eventually she was caught and put on trial. Due to the fact that she has the ability to create and control ice and cold she was sentenced to fifteen years in Prison City. She had arrived at the same time I came, about a month ago. There was also an underlying psychological problem which her family tried to keep hidden for years but had come out recently. People theorize that she had a mental break which led to her crime spree.

After a bit our food arrives and it looks quite amazing, certainly not the thirty dollars the whole thing is worth. I grabbed my burger and bit into it. It is delicious and I know I will be coming back sooner than I thought I would. I look over at Freeza and realize she is cutting a slice in her steak. But next is something I can't believe. She sticks her finger in the slice and instantly I can see cool air radiate from her finger and then from the cut in her steak.

"What are you doing?" I ask slightly whispering.

"It's a neat trick I learned," she responds in a whisper. "I can get my meal for free if they think it wasn't cooked thoroughly," she snickers. "If you want I can do the same for your burger." I am floored. It's a good burger so why would I want to ruin it so I didn't have to pay. I shook my head and she just shrugged but soon enough signals to the waiter. He hurries over.

"Is anything wrong ma'am?" He asks quite concerned that he is being called over.

She pulls herself up and speaks in an official tone. "I don't know what type of place this is but when I order a steak I expect it to be actually cooked. Feel it!" she grabs his hand and puts it on the steak. After a second he pulls his hand away like it was attacking him.

"I am so sorry, let me take that from you." He grabs the plate and turns to leave but that's as far as I could let him go.

"Wait, it was cooked just fine," I can't believe it the words just flew from my mouth before I could think. The waiter turns around and looks directly at me. Freeza is giving me a death stare like she doesn't believe what I am doing to her. "She has the power of cold so she used her powers to make the steak seem like it wasn't cooked. If you look at the steak its cooked fine so it shouldn't be cold." The waiter looks from me to her. Suddenly the other people around us stop talking and look towards us.

"Is this true?" the waiter asks. He looks less afraid like he might lose his job and more angry that it seems like he has been tricked. But Freeza's attention is all on me.

"You idiot you just had to say something!" she jumps from her seat and grabs for me. Instinctively I jump out of my seat and move away from her. The table upends and falls to the ground. Freeza on the other hand lands quite gracefully on her feet. She puts her hand out from her body like she is going to do something but instead the large man from the other table grabs her hand and brings both of her arms behind her back, effectively rendering her immobile and unable to do anything.

"I think we might want to escort her out of here," the man says to the woman at his table, who immediately gets up and starts pulling her out. The waiter looks terrified at me like I am going to attack him but I am just as confused. Less than a second after they left the bouncer appears and starts talking to the waiter who told him the story. The bouncer walks up to me.

"I am sorry sir but I am going to have to have you leave." He grabs me by my arm and I instinctively use a shadow hand to push him away. What I didn't mean to happen is for him to fly into the wall that is next to my table and fall onto the mess that was all over the floor from my table being upended.

Everyone is now staring at me ready to fight me if necessary. But I just don't want to be there. "I know, I know, I am leaving." And that is just what I do. I leave that place disappointed at the way the night happened.

CHAPTER 7

Present day.
"She is not my girlfriend. She never has been and never will be." I know it is just a joke but it always irks me the way he jokes about it. I look in the room from behind our door and I notice that the walls are radiating coolness and icicles are slightly forming on the ceiling. Freeza is in the middle of a mental episode. She seems to lose control of her powers when she is in an episode.

"How do you want to proceed?" he unsheathes his daggers and has them ready.

"Just confront her. If I am right she is in the middle of a break so nothing is going to work except confronting her." I stand up and push open the remains of the door. She is facing "The Frozen Abyss" and I can understand why she could be here. She is "The Freeze Queen of Prison City". Of course she wants the painting. Freeza is one of the rogues of the city. She mostly just thinks for herself and never for anyone else. She's not a part of any gangs. We have confronted each other plenty of times before now. "Hello, Freeza." I say. She turns around and I am not surprised to see a piercing smile on her face.

"Why Devon it's been awhile since I've seen your face. How long has it been since our last encounter?" Her voice has such a high tone to it, like a little girl that just got her hand caught in the cookie jar and is trying to act innocent.

"About two months. Adelina, what are you doing here?" her face has a momentary flash of anger but she recovers quickly.

"Please, Devon, it's Freeza. As to what I am doing here, isn't it obvious? I want 'The Frozen Abyss'," she turns around to face it, "It's such a pretty piece of artwork and since it isn't for sale I will just have to take it."

Sheamus then steps up beside me. "Now, Freeza, this isn't the way to do this. Maybe you should just come with us?" She turns around to us and she doesn't look all that happy with his statement.

"Sheamus just shut up. Me and Devy here were talking and you just need to go away!" Suddenly she creates an ice disk in her hand and throws it directly at Devon's chest. Without flinching he raises one of his daggers and the disk hits it and is deflected off towards the side with no damage done to him.

I, on the other hand, add myself in quickly and wrap a shadow whip around one of Freeza's arms. I approach her a bit and have her face me. She still looks to be quite angry at the situation.

"Why are you always around him? I love you. You and me should be together!" she screams at me with the last part. This is a common theme. She is quite jealous of Sheamus and is jealous of our partnership.

"You make it seem like Sheamus and I are in a relationship. We are partners to take down people like you. He's not the problem, you are." She doesn't like that. She immediately recoils her hand and I know what is coming. I un-coil the whip from her arm and jump back as a cold blast comes from her hand and hits the area I was just in. She then creates two long icicles and holds them like swords. Sheamus immediately comes in front of me with his daggers raised in front of him.

"Freeza, don't do this. You need to get help." Freeza becames enraged by the sight of Sheamus and starts lashing out with her icicles. Sheamus tries to defend himself and it seems like a stalemate but Sheamus is obviously not using everything he has to offer. Freeza then raises her leg and kicks Sheamus straight in his chest knocking him back. She turns towards me and tries to stab me with one of the icicles but I raise up a shadow wall in-between us. But that action just makes her attack the wall more.

"Bitch," I mumble under my breath. With that her icicles break and she is standing there without a weapon. I push the wall at her which dazes her from the slight impact and pushes her back a bit. I take up a fighting stance while standing my ground in case she comes after me but I don't have to worry. Sheamus, from behind her, grabs her hands and holds them behind her back effectively keeping her immobile. I put my hands down and walk over to them. Freeza is struggling but doesn't have the strength Sheamus has.

"Good job, Sheamus." Those are probably the wrong words to use in this situation since Freeza's eyes narrowed and she looks even madder now.

"But. I. Love. You!" She then lets out a blast of cold from her hands breaking free of Sheamus's grasp and freezing his feet to the ground. She comes up to me and before I can prepare myself she punches me in the face and runs out the door. I am able to compose myself quickly even though my face hurts quite a bit. For a tiny woman she can be brutal. I move towards Sheamus but he immediately puts out his hands.

"I can easily get out of this," he removes a dagger from his sheath, "go after her, she can't get away in the state she is in." I agree with his assessment. She is more dangerous during her mental episodes. I head out the door, but now the battle is much more dangerous.

CHAPTER 8

I rush outside and the first thing I can hear is cackling. Well it is more like laughter, but it isn't a pleasant laughing. Even though it is night I can see just fine since there is a full moon out. I scan the surroundings as quickly as possible. On my left is the decorative pond that is full of water. I note to myself to stay away from the area since it would give her more leverage and weapons. To my right is a walkway that heads towards the forest that is the entrance to the area. I scan around but can't seem to find her. I can hear her but can't see her, until she comes around the side of the building that is closest to the forest. She has a crazed look on her face. It is a combination of happy and slightly intoxicated. I am now on my guard. At this point I'm not sure what can happen.

"Come on, Devy-poo. Let's have some fun. Want to dance? Let's dance." With that she starts running at me, using her hands to release cold blasts at me and freezing the ground in front of me a bit. I retaliate by using a shadow hand to grab at a ledge above me and pull myself up and away from her attacks. I push myself off from the building and land a few feet away from her with her back to me. I then kick her square in the back which knocks her down on her knees.

"Why!" she screams, yelling it straight at the ground. I never make it a thing to try and understand what is going on inside her head at any given moment.

"You need to calm down." I am giving her a chance which is more than she deserves.

"No!" she whips her head to face me and launches a cold blast at my face. Luckily, I manage to bring up a small shadow wall to protect my face except for a small bit that hit me and freezes some of my hair. No damage has been done except for discomfort. Well, except the fact that I react by losing my balance and falling straight to the ground.

Freeza leaps from where she is and lands on top of me and starts hitting my chest with her hands. "You. Love. Me!" I am not a fan of getting hit and in reaction pull up a small wall between the two of us and push it away from me.

Good news. This gets Freeza off of me.

Bad news. I launch her too far and she ends up landing in the pond I specifically told myself to stay away from. Now I am in for a fight. I scramble to get back to my feet just in time to see Freeza blast out of the pond and into the air. With that the pond instantly freezes with a column of ice jetting up in the center about twenty feet high. Almost gracefully she lands on the top of it, still sporting a crazy smile. I groan at the sight.

"Bitch."

"Come on, Devy, we still need to dance." She then starts throwing ice disks at me from atop her pillar. I have to jump or duck out of the way of each one that comes from her to keep it from hitting me. These are insanely accurate. After about seven have been thrown I have positioned myself just close enough that I throw out a shadow whip and get it wrapped around her leg. Using momentum from running I pull her from her pedestal. She falls but only for a foot or so until she recovers and using cold beams she is able to draw out an ice slide that she uses to direct a path down safely. A path that I am directly in front of.

I dive out of the way as Freeza slides on her ice right past me. I jump up and she lands a few meters from me looking fine. I, on the other hand am dirty and winded from all the running and getting hit.

"Can we stop this? You need help." It is a futile attempt at stopping the situation but it is the best I have.

"Why stop? I am having fun, Devy-poo. I'm having so much fun with our dancing." She gets two more disks in her hand and throws them at me. I am quick though and dodge out of the way. She makes two disks and throws them at me, but I am one step ahead of her. I create a shadow hand and dodge out of the way of one, using my hand to catch the second one. Then I throw it right back at her. Shock registers on her face as she ducks out of the way just in time. Looking at the disk fly away she looks back at me with a look of pure death. It is not the reaction I was expecting. Actually, I was more expecting to hit her.

"That was a mistake!" she screams creating one more ice disk and throwing it at me. I am not expecting it and so it hits me directly in my left shoulder and knocks me down on the ground. The pain is awful for some solid water that hit me. I know in the morning it would be incredibly sore and maybe still painful. That bitch! After a few seconds of rubbing my shoulder I look up and realize that I am in more danger than I thought.

I am only a few feet from the edge of the pond.

Is this part of some twisted plan in her mind? No, I am convinced she has no idea what she is doing. She is in no mental state to be able to make a good plan of defeating me. I scramble to my feet and realize just how bad it is going to be for me. Freeza is running right at me and in a second jumps up with her feet extended in front of her and hits me square in the chest.

I guess I have more things to worry about than my shoulder.

I fly through the air and land right on the frozen pond. I am dazed, winded and my shoulder is killing me but I know I have to get off this pond. I try getting up but getting traction on this ice is more difficult than I expected and I keep slipping. Finally, I am able to get to my feet and stay standing after a few seconds. But I find Freeza standing at the edge as well. Smiling.

"We could've had so much fun." She then raises her hands and my feet are surrounded by ice blocks, cementing them in place. I try moving but I can't lift my feet. Panic then sets in. "Don't worry, we'll see each other in about sixty years when I am done with this drab world. Goodbye, Devy" With that she puts her hand on the ice in front of her and the ice on the pond starts to melt. The frozen pond and even the column. All of it, except my ice boots. I throw out a shadow whip to grab hold of her but at that moment I fall through the ice, my whip goes wild and I start sinking to the bottom of the pond.

It is probably a good ten feet deep but it is just as scary to be that far away from air. I struggle all I can to break free from the ice but I can't. I use shadow hands to try and pull myself up but I can't get a grasp onto anything. My throat is starting to burn and I know I don't have much time left. I look up above and notice someone diving into the pond and swimming down towards me. My vision is fading but I can tell it is Sheamus.

Using a dagger he immediately starts chipping away at an ice block and in only three strikes the block crumbles away. He then grabs me around my arms and pulls me up. While it is a struggle for him it is a lot easier with one ice block attached to me and not two and I am able to swim a bit to help. Soon enough our heads break the water's surface and we gasp for air, me more than him, while trying to get to the edge of the pond. We drag ourselves back onto land and I lie on the ground while Sheamus uses the dagger to chip away at the remaining ice block.

"Where's Freeza?" I say in between trying to get my breath back. Sheamus sits next to me cross legged.

"I'm not sure. I saw her drop you into the water through the front window of the museum and then she ran off. I got out here as quickly as possible and dove in the water." Gosh it feels like I have been in the water for a while but apparently it was only less than thirty seconds. I guess the concept of dying makes time slow down. Who knew?

"That bitch tries to kill me and doesn't even see it through. How nice." I sit back up, as recovered as I can be. We are both soaking wet. "So what's the count of us saving each other?" Sheamus smiles.

"I think I've saved you eighty-five times and you've saved me fifty-three times."

"Did you make those numbers up?" I ask.

"Of course. But the concept is all the same. You owe me big time." He chuckles at that.

"OK, OK." I am suddenly quite exhausted and my shoulder is very sore now. "Let's just go home." We both get up and start walking home. Tomorrow is going to be an exceptionally difficult day.

CHAPTER 9

*T*he day after a fight is worse than the fight itself. Why? Because the damage you get is felt all at once. That remains true after my fight with Freeza. I wake up and my shoulder feels awful. My feet strangely feel a tad raw probably from the ice blocks they were stuck in.

I, as gently as I can, get out of bed and walk out of my room. At this moment Sheamus exits his room and looks exhausted and seems to be limping. Since his legs and feet were affected by the ice longer than my feet were it must feel worse. We both move towards the living room and sit down on the couch. We don't say anything for a few moments, just trying to salvage as much not moving as possible. Considering that we are both in just boxer shorts, our injuries are quite apparent. I have a bruise on my shoulder and my chest. Sheamus has a small bruise on his chest where Freeza kicked him. Both of our feet and Sheamus's legs look pale from the ice. I decide to speak first.

"So as much as I don't want to say it and would love to just continue sitting here, we do have to go after her." Sheamus groans and then winces from groaning.

"I know, and we have so much we have to do. We need to update Scotty and visit Freeza's psychiatrists as well as her apartment. Plus guard the museum again if we don't find Freeza today." It didn't hit me until now how much we have to do and it is only eight-thirty in the morning. I decide to take the plunge.

"Ok I am going to get dressed for the day." I get off the couch (with some minor difficulty and Sheamus doing a bit of pushing) and start to leave the room.

"Hey Devon."

"Yea?" I stop before I leave the room.

"Can you go into my room and just give me some clothes so I can get dressed out here and not have to move much?" I laugh and wince.

"Of course."

* * *

Half an hour later we are on our way to the museum. It is drizzling by the time we arrive. Both of us are wearing jeans and a windbreaker. His is red and mine is black. We look around at the museum property. Even though it is drizzling there is too much water and mud on the lawn to have been done from just light rain and it's obvious it was from the battle that happened last night. The leftover ice must have melted from the summer heat and left what we see here: a mess.

"This wasn't our fault," Sheamus states. I just chuckle and walk over to the pond where the last part of the night happened.

I look at it remembering just how insane Freeza was by the end. She was willing to literally drown me. Apparently her insanity made her love for me want to also hurt, brutalize or even kill me. But I've been in quite a few perilous situations before so I don't hang on to it that much.

But that isn't the reason I am so intent on looking in this pond. Something about it is getting to me and I can't be sure what.

"We might as well get this over with." Sheamus says coming up behind me.

We enter the museum and the first thing I hear is someone ranting their head off about something. I recognize the voice as Scotty instantly. We follow the sounds until we reach the room that held the precious works of art that are all paintings, the exact same room that started the fighting from yesterday.

It is soaking wet all around our feet, once again another unfortunate problem from our fight last night. The damage that can happen afterwards we don't exactly think about. Thankfully none of the paintings or other artworks look damaged and only the floor is covered in water. But that doesn't stop us from getting the brunt force of blame. I can tell because Scotty is looking at us with fire in his eyes.

"You two! What the hell happened here last night?" Scotty immediately ran and sloshed his way over to us, by the time he is across the room his brilliant tan suit is soaked from the knees down. We quickly explain everything that happened the night before.

"We didn't mean to leave a flood like this. We were just trying to stop Freeza from stealing your painting. Of course like everything else she always makes things difficult in the long run for everyone," I state to Scotty. He seems to calm down after hearing what we went through and honestly looks worried about our wellbeing but doesn't look like he is going to pry into it all.

"Ahhh the famed ice princess. The psycho-ess of Prison City. I haven't heard about her getting into trouble lately. Kind of wish she didn't want anything to do with me though." Didn't he know it. Usually Freeza had some psycho plan cracked up, I would take her down and then someone else in the city had to find some way to clean up the damage she caused. Not many people like her even when she isn't having one of her episodes.

"Can we help?" Sheamus asks. I hope he will say no because we have enough on our plates and I don't want to have to be tied up anymore with using a mop to clean up a lot of water.

"No it's okay. I'll do it along with some staff to help out. We'll get it done. Just make sure you stop her from coming back tonight." We promise and tell him if need be we would be coming back tonight to do more guard duty. We leave the museum just as a janitor is coming in with a mop and bucket. Thankfully we don't have to do any of that.

"I guess next up is the mental hospital to report this to her psychiatrists," Sheamus says as we walk down the hill from the museum.

"Let's also hope we run into Freeza along the way and wrap this up once and for all," I say really wanting to have my wish come true.

CHAPTER 10

Sadly my wish isn't granted and our walk to the hospital is uneventful. The rain stops by the time we leave the museum and it is just overcast now. When we walk up to the three story building it looks eerie. Even though it is daylight out it is a creepy building to look at. About a fifth of the windows are broken, vines are crawling up the building and occasionally you can hear screaming happening from inside. It reminds me of an old timey asylum you see in horror movies. Except this one isn't abandoned. Freeview Mental Hospital is the only place in the city where extreme mental disorders are to be treated. If you are lucky you get to stay here for as long as you are a prisoner or until your disorder gets cleared up. If you aren't so lucky, like with Freeza, you are allowed to have regular visits with psychiatrists to make sure you aren't on the decline or a danger. Freeza is classified as having episodes of psychosis so considering that some of the time she is completely fine she isn't allowed to stay here, even though many prisoners would love to keep her there.

"Dr. Anes and Dr. Freeview are the psychiatrists assigned to her still, right?" I ask Sheamus.

"Yup, they haven't gone anywhere." Like with the rest of the jobs in the prison that isn't security for the prison, the doctors are inmates. Prisoners are treating prisoners. Thankfully, doctors can be criminals as well. The hospital is understaffed but still thankfully they have enough to get by.

We walk into the mental hospital and are immediately overwhelmed with the amount of activity that is going on. This is just the entrance area where major hallways intersect with each other to leave the building. There are four patients being attended by three doctors and two nurses. This is the exact definition of understaffed. The two nurses are trying to get the four patients, three guys and one woman, under control. The doctors are using their mostly mental based powers on the patients. We don't have time for that and just walk around them to the front desk. The man at the desk looks terrified by the commotion going on a few feet from him, but quickly tries to look as professional as possible when looking at us.

"Is Dr. Anes or Dr. Freeview in?" Sheamus asks the man.

"Uhhh yes and no. What I mean is," his eyes shift over as one of the patients screams and slumps over on the ground, "Dr. Anes isn't here but Dr. Freeview is in her office. Room 317." One of the doctors heaves the patient up over his shoulder and our nervous looking man looks scared for his life.

"Thank you," Sheamus says, as we walk toward the elevator to get to Dr. Freeview.

This isn't our first time here. Thankfully, we've never been here as patients. We get to the elevators after a nice walk down a long and boring corridor. Once on the third floor we are looking less stressed. It never makes us feel ok to be in a place where everyone is a super-powered psycho that can just come at us at any time against us. We walk up to room 317 and I knock on the open door and Dr. Freeview looks at us.

Dr. Jane Freeview is in her early 40's, is average height but is tall in high heels and has long brown hair and piercing green eyes. She is wearing a plain pink shirt with a blue plaid skirt and red glasses. The many times I've seen her, I always think if she stopped being a psychiatrist she could easily be a librarian. But that can never happen since the "Freeview" in Freeview Mental Hospital refers to her. She came to the prison roughly six years ago and immediately went to help in the hospital and was such a stunning improvement to the patients that the previous head named the hospital after her and promptly quit and gave her that job. Now she only takes on no more than ten patients, and one of them is Freeza, her personal challenge. Her power is the ability to experience the memories of others and see what it was like for them. Using a power like that can make being a physiatrist easier but using it has to be done within an official capacity. A few times she didn't get the correct documentation, signed or even permission, that's why she is in here with us.

Looking at us she doesn't look especially happy.

"Please Devon tell me you've gone off the deep end and want to be admitted. Please tell me that's why you are here."

"No, Jane, it's Freeza again. She's back at it."

* * *

We finish telling Jane the story of what we went through last night over bottles of water. The more we tell her the more she looks like she is going to blow a gasket.

"She has been doing well for two months. TWO MONTHS. Why now of all times did she decide to relapse? I was just feeling ok with maybe cutting back on her therapy to once a week instead of three times a week."

"Last time I saw her was the dismantling of the pride statue in the park. She really wasn't a fan of Master Pride," I state, remembering the incident vividly.

"She was bouncing off the walls. To think all Pride did to piss her off was tell her that building an ice fortress in the middle of a forest was wrong. That was almost a year ago and she decided to wait nine months just to get revenge." She drinks from her water bottle and sets it down on her desk rather roughly. "She has been one of the most challenging patients I've ever had. I have no clue what sets her off. It's almost like she wakes up and decides to be angry at someone or want something or do whatever the hell she wants. Then she can easily be put in a correct state of mind the next day." This is the truest statement I have ever heard. Her wants and ideas are so bizarre even I can't follow them. Plus when she is in a mental episode she has this undying need to be in love with me but at the same time try and knock me unconscious with an ice ball.

"We just wanted to warn you about all this because if we catch her, which should be either today or tomorrow, you will need to be notified about getting her from wherever we are to the hospital," Sheamus adds in not wanting to put added stress of rehashing the past for the both of us. Usually what happens is that I knock her down in a fight and the cavalry comes in from the hospital to pick her up and transport her there to stay for a period of time.

"Well thank you both. I'm sorry you once again have to get dragged into her mess but you are the best ones for the job." We all stand up at that point since the conversation is over.

"Don't be sorry, it isn't your fault," I say as we walk out. They both know what I mean. It wasn't Jane's fault that Freeza keeps relapsing into the torrent of annoyance and destruction she is. It is Freeza's fault and I make sure to keep that front and center.

CHAPTER 11

We leave the hospital and start our fifteen minute walk to Freeza's apartment since the only other person that could know about Freeza's mindset the past couple of days is her roommate, Casey Daskel. Casey is another informant for Sheamus. Her only job for Sheamus is to keep us updated on how Freeza is acting and if to notify us if there are any trouble signs. Her power is that she is incredibly good with being in touch with a person's emotions. A stupid crime and a city notorious on putting super-powered criminals in Prison City was how she landed here. But her power makes her really useful in keeping in tune with Freeza and how she is doing. She has been doing that for practically a year and a half, once we started realizing Freeza was trouble. She hasn't warned us of anything so we are pretty sure she doesn't know of anything that has happened.

We know the way and so we are there promptly at 11:15 knocking on the door that contains the two bedroom apartment. The door opens up to show us a girl in a pink bra and grey sweatpants. Her blond hair and face make it look like we just woke her up. But the sound that comes out of her mouth indicates to us that she is now awake.

"She's not here and because you both are here it means she's flipped again. Perfect. Get in here." We walk into the living room which has green wallpaper on the walls. Sheamus and I head for the couch while Casey goes into another room. It is only a minute of waiting before she comes back out now wearing a light cream colored t-shirt. She sits down on a chair opposite from us.

"Should we go through the story?" Sheamus asks.

"Don't bother. I'll hear about it around town soon enough. I just woke up and honestly I haven't seen her since 6 last night. I thought she might have gone to some party. I went to bed early since I was awake almost thirty hours prior to that." That explains the more than twelve hours of sleep it looks like she received.

"Do you think she might have figured out you were connected to me?" Sheamus asks. Casey gives us a snort like it is a joke.

"No way. I'm awesome at my job. I act like a party girl. I am employed to organize some of the best parties in this city for people. I basically shave off twenty IQ points around her just for show. There is no way she could have figured it out. Plus she didn't go after me did she? That's why you are here. She went after something or someone else." She has a good point. Her cover wasn't blown.

"How's her job doing?" Sheamus asks. Freeza is a fashion columnist for the Prison City Magazine, a magazine that dedicates itself to talking about gossip in the city and other not newsworthy subjects that couldn't go into the official newspaper.

"Her job seems to be going fine. She's constantly going out and taking pictures of what people are wearing then going back into her room to write up her opinions for her column," Casey states. Sheamus just gives a hum at the information, probably not seeing anything unusual or interesting about it.

"Ok but just notify us if she comes back. Plus contact Dr. Freeview or the hospital if you see her around."

"No problem, just make sure she doesn't cause any more damage. I have to keep my reputation as sparkly as possible and I would rather people not start thinking I might be connecting to her more than just splitting rent."

* * *

We arrive back at our apartment a bit after twelve, after going through the people we have to notify about Freeza's escapades. We fall back on the couch exhausted after not being able to give our bodies the proper rest and recovery they deserve. We also know they weren't going to get anymore tonight since we have to be back at the museum to guard it the best we can.

"So what are your thoughts?" Sheamus asks me.

"Well I don't know why she decided to steal a painting out of the blue but I am ninety-five percent sure that we will see her at the museum again tonight. Probably wanting to steal the painting again or hoping I will be there. Either way we'll be there to stop her." Of all the villains I face here, Freeza can be the most tiring one. Her reasons for causing destruction are just all over the place and her intense expression of her love for me is, just nutty.

"Even though I will be there with you, be careful. She's off the wall now and who knows how far she is willing to go when fighting with her." I understand what he means. I'm not sure what her motives will be if we see her there again. It seems like last night she came for the painting but as time went on she just wanted to do battle with me and only me. Which reminds me about Sheamus.

"You need to be careful as well. You know she's jealous of our partnership and has no problem with doing either of us harm but more so against you she won't hold back," I state to him. He only nods.

This is the problem with rogue people. Sometimes you just can't figure out their motivation. With the gangs, someone is in charge and they usually stuck to the plan. With one insane person it is hard to figure out just what motivates them and how they will react to a change in their plan. Such as two meddlesome defenders crashing their party.

"We'll leave here the same time as last night and try to stick to a similar plan. I don't want her getting the upper hand on us. Especially me." While Sheamus is a capable fighter with weapons and his fists, it still isn't practical for him to be facing a psycho that could freeze him in an instant. That's why I am such a good partner for him. Having tangible fighting powers keeps the pressure off of him and lets him be able to do his planning stuff.

"Don't worry, I'll keep you safe," I smile and try to stand up but immediately fall back on the couch. "Maybe we should take it as easy as possible before we go. At least rest up and heal as best as we can."

"My thoughts exactly," he says.

CHAPTER 12

We each take a five hour nap after our talk to try and recuperate as best as possible. After awakening and eating dinner we talk and get a good battle plan ready. While it is just an outline since most plans always change we know the basics of what we should be doing. By the time night rolls around we are ready to depart and get ready for what is next. We are both dressed in black t-shirts and grey jeans. We look like robbers in the night. The only difference between the two of us is that Sheamus is wearing a sort of holster that holds two batons which are rigged to heat to very high temperatures. Sheamus planned ahead in case he had to go toe to toe with Freeza or she freezes him on the spot again. Sadly, my shadows don't get hot but I work with them well.

"Ready?" he asks as we make sure we are ready to leave.

"As ready as I'll ever be," I say. With that we leave the apartment and head on our way back to the museum. Back to certain hell...except it isn't going to be as hot.

As dangerous of a place Prison City is you don't feel all that endangered when you are walking alone at night. Small time crimes like muggings and out of the place beatings don't really happen since everyone has powers and you don't want to fight someone if you don't know what they can do to you. Plus knowing our reputation no one is going to just come after us randomly in the night. We can hear a couple of parties in the distance, some yelling coming from a house close to us and surprisingly what sounds like a bottle being dropped on the ground around us.

"Gosh the city is alive tonight," Sheamus says to me.

"Yea but none of it is our problem tonight. Who needs parties when we can fight a psycho ice queen?" Sheamus laughs at me. I smile a bit. Usually

I'm not such a downer when it comes to doing things here but Freeza just sets me off and I hate dealing with her. Sheamus always keeps me as grounded as possible when dealing with her.

The rest of the time we keep going over a game plan but soon enough our plan has to be put in motion as we arrive at the dimly lit museum. I look over at the pond and get another bad feeling about it.

"You know how much I hate that pond?" I ask Sheamus.

"I mean you almost drowned in it. I would have problems with any type of body of water for a bit after that. A little worrying over a pond never harmed anyone. Now we need to get inside." I follow Sheamus as he once again unlocks the front door, enters and locks the door behind us. Everything looks the same as the night before. Dimly lit and quiet. We walk back into the main area of the museum and decide to check in on the painting art work area that we were sure Freeza would be in. As Sheamus and I approach the door I silently hope she won't be there in a surprise ambush for us. He opens the door and I breathe a sigh of relief seeing no one in the room with us. It is empty and surprisingly dry. The maintenance staff certainly knows how to clean up water efficiently.

"I guess the coast is clear," he says and I only hope it stays that way for the rest of the night. Seeing no one else would make my week right now.

"Do you think we should just stay here or patrol the rest of the museum?" I ask.

"I think we should stay here for a little while and wait to see if she shows her face. I honestly don't believe she is looking to rob anything except the painting here but I think her true motivation is probably us or mainly you." I agree with that statement. I am always on her radar and now that she knows I was onto what she is doing she is probably even more motivated to come here but the reason for coming has changed.

"I say we should give her ten minutes. I don't think she will take longer than that if she understands the way we work. She has been around us for the past two years." I am correct about the ten minutes part.

Five minutes later we hear the loud banging of a door being thrown open. We stand frozen to the spot as we watch the door in front of us and just wait for the moment it opens and all hell will break loose on us. We are right about the door opening. It opens and there is Freeza, looking at us with a crazed look in her eyes, a smile as wide as her whole face, and her hair looks all out of place and has small crystals of ice forming on the ends. I was wrong about all hell breaking loose on us part though. She is just standing there looking at us.

"Awww lovebug you showed up to our date," she says before she turns to look at Sheamus and immediately scowls, "I didn't know you were bringing the mite along as well."

"Freeza, stop this you are having one of your episodes. You need to go to Freeview." This is going to be the only chance I would give her to reason with us to do this simply.

"Oh Devy you are right we should watch some sort of TV show together. But first we need to get rid of your little shadow," she says. She puts her hands out aiming at Sheamus. But I am not going to let her get the first shot on us.

"Wait I have one simple question for you." She puts her hands down to her sides and looks at me with the greatest smile ever knowing I am giving her attention now. "Where have you been all day?" It is a simple question and I know she would understand what I am asking.

"Why I think you knew. You looked at me twice today. I was in the pond all night and all day." Of course it makes sense why I kept looking at the pond. She probably formed an ice bubble around herself to hide. She has done it once before but has never mastered it quite right and I must have put it out of my mind until now. Sheamus looks over at me.

"Next time you have a feeling about something and I put it off as fear you are completely allowed to hit me," Sheamus whispers to me.

"What was that you little cockroach?" Freeza screams at him. Her hands blast out some frost which covers the ground around her in ice. Sheamus becomes frightened from the outburst and quickly draws his batons and faces her.

"Wait wait wait," I quickly say to her. I need to prolong this fight as much as possible until I can figure out a way to quickly bring her down. "How exactly did you get into the museum? We locked the door behind us."

"Why sweetie I never told you. I have a lock picking set. I can easily open locked doors." Well damn I never knew about that. Little rich girl has got some street tricks to her. "Now I need to take care of your friend so we can actually go on our date now."

Damn I guess that is as much prolonging as I can do. This is when all hell breaks loose on us.

CHAPTER 13

Freeza sends out a blast of cold air directly at Sheamus and I am quick to bring up a wall between it and him. She lets loose a combination of a growl and a scream after seeing her attack not hurt him. This time though she starts running at him with a crazed look about her. Sheamus is already ready in a fighting stance against her with his batons. She throws a punch at him but he easily blocks it by raising his arm. She tries kicking at his legs but he easily jumps to avoid her attack. She isn't using her powers but is trying for hand-to-hand combat against him. That is a mistake on her part, but insanity won't let you think clearly.

He quickly brings both batons down on her shoulders and that knocks her feet from under her, slumping her to the floor. She doesn't seem hurt for long as she crawls away quickly and gets right back up. If she keeps this up I wouldn't have to be worried that much about him fighting her. What I am worried about was that we both aren't at a hundred percent. I am hoping that won't be a problem for us.

Freeza seems to slightly understand what is going on and uses her hands to send out a blast of cold directly at Sheamus. I am prepared to protect him but I don't need to. He puts up his batons directly in front of him and the blast and the cold air sort of dissipates once it is around the batons. Of course. At some point he must have turned on the heat and now has a bit more protection against her ice attacks. At this stage I decide to help out my partner.

I rush into the fight to form a triangle being between Sheamus and Freeza. I send out a shadow hand to try and knock Freeza off balance and hopefully knock her down long enough to gain the upper hand. She ducks around my attack and throws an ice ball at me which I easily duck out of the way from in return. I look at Sheamus and nod at him, indicating to him to get close to me.

I decide to do some rapid fire whip attacks on her to keep her at a distance and maybe be able to talk to Sheamus. While I let loose a barrage of attacks to keep her at bay, Sheamus makes his way over to me.

"I'll box her in on the other side and that way we have a better chance of ending this quickly." I nod while making sure Freeza doesn't get a chance to counterattack. With Sheamus trying to get to the other side of Freeza I attack a bit more efficiently. I let her think that I am slowing down my attacks and let her counter attack. She buys it and quickly lets loose a couple of ice balls in my general direction. I switch to a shadow hand, in order to maintain a good defense, and I am able to grab one of the balls and throw it back at her. I am hoping to hit her legs but instead I throw it a bit low and it hits the ground. It shatters, sending ice everywhere. One of the shards gets underneath one of her feet and she slips on it and falls down. Sheamus is now behind her, between her and the door. We effectively have her boxed in with no means of escape and she has been knocked down. I'm not sure how long we can hold this up, but we are doing quite well now.

"Freeza it's over you should just give up now and let us get you to the hospital." What I don't tell her is that we would be bringing in a bunch of people to transport her rather than personally bringing her.

"No no no get away from me!" She sends out blasts of cold air from her hands in just random directions and not at either of us. Now she is desperate, and she knows it "Devy, please don't do this to your one true love." She looks at me with pleading eyes and a whine in her voice. I see Sheamus slowly walking up behind her with sheathed batons.

"It has to be done for everyone's sake." At that moment Sheamus grabs Freeza by her arms and holds her as tightly as possible so she can't get away. She screams for dear life and struggles as best as she can but Sheamus is stronger than her. What Sheamus isn't as ready for is the blast of cold air that comes from her hands that startles him and makes him lose his grip on her. He shakes off the ice that forms on his arms and she quickly runs off forming a sort of ice trail that she is able to slide on out of the room.

"Damn I had her," Sheamus curses. I'm not giving up that easily. She isn't going to let me lose another twenty-four hours of my life worrying about when she will appear next.

"We still have her. Call Dr. Freeview and get her and her team here. I am going to try and keep her here." I run off after her. Sheamus behind me tells me to be careful. I hope I won't have to mind being careful. I am hoping she will be too deranged to even want to harm me.

CHAPTER 14

I follow the trail of ice outside and see Freeza at the end of the pathway looking around trying to find a way to escape. Or she looks like someone is about to pounce on her.

"Freeza, don't run," I tell her. She turns around looking terrified but soon the look of fear turns into a look of malice. Evil and revengeful. A smile that an evil dictator would feel fearful of.

"Now Devy. Cutiepie. Why would I want to run from you? We are meant to be together." Damnit when will I ever get a break from this intense need to love me? I get into a fighting stance and she does the same.

She sends out cold air from her hands and I think it could be an attack on me but she aims it directly at the ground. Then she jumps and slides on it and creates another ice path. This one is used to get behind me. I am prepared for a fight though. I use shadow whips to try and trip her up on her ice path. None of them are effective but at least I am more prepared. She can't seem to find a good place to stop without me being able to make contact with her. So she just keeps siding around me until eventually she jumps off and starts running towards the wooded entrance. Not being able to get to her without making my way through the maze of ice around me I put up a shadow wall right in front of her. She runs right into it and falls right on her back. By the time I have maneuvered my way out of the ice she is already on her feet facing me.

"You know what this reminds me of? Our date when we were in the forest. All nice and icy and just the two of us." She throws an ice ball at me and I block it with a wall.

"You mean the time when you created an ice fortress in the middle of the forest and I had to drag you out from there. It took so long not only to melt the ice but to be able to repair the damage to the forest."

"Ahhh, but what about our date up on the transmission tower? That was lovely being able to look out around the city." Bitch.

"The time you thought that maybe you could send your ice out throughout the city through radio waves and freeze everyone listening to you," Seriously did we ever experience the same stuff?

"The nice date in Daniel Foster's backyard?"

"You held him hostage because you thought he was the devil and wanted to steal my soul."

"Well, who asked you?" She screams at me. She throws another half dozen ice balls at me which I am able to dodge. She is coming more and more unhinged and with her reality spiraling out of control, so is her aim. She quickly turns away from me and heads towards the entrance to the woods again but I use a whip to grab her ankle and trip her up. She looks back at me and with rage in her eyes and she grabs my whip with her hands and freezes it. With a simple closing of her hands it shatters.

That's not good. I am not helping my situation by making her more angry.

"As much as I love you, you are really a thorn in my side." She slowly gets to her feet while I maintain eye contact with her. I am not sure if she is going to run or confront me. She then faces me, staring me down. I guess running is out of the question for her now. She puts her hands out in front of her and starts letting loose cold blasts at me using one hand at a time. She is walking towards me while I walk backwards ducking my body out of the way of what she is unleashing on me.

"This really doesn't help anyone," I state hoping that anything I say may just calm her down.

"It certainly is making me happy." Before she can attack once more, Sheamus comes out of nowhere and smacks her right in the face with his batons. She screams from the pain and is thrown down to the ground. Sheamus steadies himself and stands next to me.

"Backup is arriving soon." Music to my ears. I see him click on the switches on each baton and realize that he didn't burn her. But now he is ready for anything she can throw at him. She looks up, rubbing her face, and instead of crying from pain she looks pissed off. Damn does the bitch ever calm down?

"I am so tired of you good-for-nothing wannabe hero. You think you are so perfect but you won't take the spotlight away from my Devon." She puts her hands to the ground and ice starts to travel towards the both of us. I can tell her intention was to either to freeze both of our legs to get away or to just freeze Sheamus and keep me for herself. Sheamus quickly jumps back while I use a shadow hand and start punching at the ground and the ice coming towards us. The punches start breaking up the ground and ice which results in the flow not being as continuous and her having to keep restarting, which is frustrating her. Every time I disrupt her path she yells out in frustration. I then notice that Sheamus is making a wide circle around her. I decide to keep up my form of frustrating her so that Sheamus can get a surprise attack on her.

But it isn't enough.

"I know what you are doing you fool." She turns to look directly at Sheamus and creates a skinny ice wall in front of herself and shoves it directly towards him. Sheamus is prepared though, thankfully the wall is only the height of Freeza and so he is able to leap over it with ease. He then brings out his batons and starts swinging them at Freeza. In order to block his attacks she covers her arms in a thick ice and uses them as protection against his attack. But I notice they start turning to liquid after a while since the batons are producing heat. She notices that as well and decides to go on the attack more. Soon the tides turn and Sheamus has to use his weapons for defense.

"Freeza!" I yell. She turns to me and it is just what I am hoping for, using her need for me as a good distraction. I use a shadow hand and quickly grab one of her ice arms and apply just enough pressure that it shatters the ice. Sheamus then comes up on her other side and, using his batons, shatters the other ice arm.

Freeza isn't happy with this outcome. She uses the hand that wasn't being grabbed by me and shoots a cold blast right at me. I quickly move out of the way, but because of the unexpectedness and closeness of the attack I lose focus on the shadow hand and it disappears thus releasing her from its grip. She then swiftly kicks Sheamus in his side and starts to run away. Sheamus is able to throw one of his batons right into Freeza's legs and trip her. I rush over to make sure she won't try running away again. I create a shadow wall and cover her lower body so she won't be able to get up. Sheamus joins me barely ten seconds later.

"Well, we have her. Now to wait for Dr. Freeview to get here to take care of her," Sheamus says. I look down and notice Freeza looks positively terrified.

"I won't go back there. I refuse to let them try and understand me. No! No!" She starts frantically struggling as much as possible. She starts firing out cold blasts from her hands but the strength of my wall holds her down. That is until one of her blasts shoots towards me and hits me right in the shoulder making me lose focus for just a second and allowing her to get free. While I recover a bit from her attack Sheamus stands in front of me to make sure she doesn't have a clear shot at attacking me. But I am the least of her worries. She is mumbling to herself and looking around like something, or in this case someone, is going to jump out at her.

I finally recover enough so that I am prepared for her. "Plan?" I ask Sheamus who is still focusing all his attention on Freeza.

"Honestly, we just keep her here until Dr. Freeview arrives."

"Then I should be able to do that." I move to go in front of him instead and form a shadow rope and let it fall to my side. Then I fling it out at her and catch her around her waist. She is caught off guard by that and throws a few ice balls at me. But with her erratic behavior it is easy to move my body out of the way so they won't hit me. Even one I hear Sheamus smacking away with his batons. After a bit, I slowly pull her closer towards me while keeping her off balanced so she wouldn't be able to attack me with increased accuracy.

"You won't be able to contain me here for long. I will escape from you," she snarls at me. Well look at that. One minute she wants to be around me every second and the next she doesn't want anything to do with me. "I can and will..." but she trails off and looks frantic in one direction as we hear the unmistakable sound of voices, footsteps, and a vehicle approaching our area.

"Well, the cavalry has arrived," Sheamus says. And not a moment too soon.

CHAPTER 15

"**N**o, I refuse." Freeza sees the group of ten psychiatric staff and Dr. Freeview coming up the hill with a large van that is for transporting dangerous patients. Freeza starts wiggling a lot but is still restrained in my rope. She isn't getting away from me that easily. She starts firing off cold blasts in random directions again. I'm not sure what she is up to but it looks like she is about to have a full on panic attack. Soon enough Dr. Freeview is in front of a line of the staff, all standing next to each other. They look like they are trying to block off access to the escape route if Freeza tries to make a break for it.

"She's all yours now," I say to the doctor. Dr. Freeview nods at Sheamus and me.

"Alright now Freeza, we can make this real simple for you if you just come along now." Dr. Freeview takes a step forward towards Freeza and Freeza freaks out.

"NO!" she screams and grabs the shadow rope in her hands and freezes it like she did before, then moves away from me, putting tension on the ice, and it shatters right in front of me. I am ready for another fight that I know is coming. Worse though is I am inclined to at least protect the other eleven people that are with us now. The more people there are around the harder it will be to protect all of them. She is my problem, so my responsibility. "I hate you!" With a mighty yell she opens her mouth and out comes a blizzard. Almost instinctively I create a shadow wall in front of the psychiatric staff who are all quite shocked at what is happening. I am having a hard time keeping the wall intact but then Freeza starts to turn towards Sheamus and me. I extend the shadow wall all around Freeza so her blizzard breath can't touch anyone.

"What the hell is going on? She's never been able to do this!" I am hoping Sheamus has some sort of answer.

"I believe her insanity has hit heightened levels. It must have allowed her to unlock an advanced part of her powers. How we will get close to her now, I'm not sure," he says looking like he is concentrating on finding a weak point. I couldn't see it. She is acting like a crazed person breathing out this blizzard in all directions. Either at my wall or up in the air. She isn't letting up.

"Too bad we can't restrain her in some way, but if I let this wall down everybody will be in danger of her attack," I mention. I notice that Sheamus suddenly lights up and looks like he has thought of something.

"Hang on one second," he says as he runs around the wall. All I am doing is hanging on. I can't do anything else. I notice he is talking to one of the psychiatric staff, is handed something and comes back to me a few seconds later. "Ok, I need you to get me over the wall without bringing it down." Now he is the crazy one.

"If I put you in with her you'll be frozen faster than a serial killer's heart during winter in Antarctica." I can't see how whatever his plan is, is somehow going to help us stop the raging lunatic in front of us.

"Just do it Devon," he says sternly. Fine, I just have to trust him. I put a shadow box in front of him and when he stands on it I raise it high enough that it would be easy for him to just climb over the wall. Once he is in the circle of the wall I only hope he knows what he is doing.

But I am not disappointed.

He jumps in right behind Freeza as she is trying to direct her blizzard breath at the psychiatric staff, but to no avail because of my wall. She seems to notice that she has company in her tiny prison area and stops her attack long enough to look at what it is. Her eyes go wide, rage fills her face, and with a startling yell she uses another blizzard breath aimed right at Sheamus. Sheamus is more prepared than she is and quickly runs around in a circle around Freeza, who follows him as closely as possible with her attack. Then in a blink of an eye Sheamus does an impressive backflip in the air above Freeza and lands perfectly behind her. Before she can even react to losing her target Sheamus shoves her to the ground, thus stopping her attack since her face hits, and takes out a pair of handcuffs and quickly cuffs Freeza's hands behind her back, thus immobilizing her on the ground.

"All clear," Sheamus says to me. I take down the wall, seeing Freeza struggling on the ground to get back to her feet. She isn't succeeding and all she is doing is getting dirty rolling around. I walk up to Sheamus with Dr. Freeview and her staff also coming up from their side.

"Good job, Sheamus. We'll take it from here." She nods to one of her staff who holds out his hands which start to glow a purplish color. That same color surrounds Freeza who is lifted in the air. She tries to struggle but it isn't effective. The man carries her into the open part of the back of the transport van and the door behind him is shut, effectively completing our mission.

"I guess you'll take her back to the hospital to try and calm her down," I say to Dr. Freeview. She looks at us after she makes sure Freeza is contained in the back of the van and nods.

"Try is the key word in this. I've never seen her this unstable before." I agree with that statement. She went over the edge this time around. "Her powers have multiplied because of this and I will need to figure out what truly set her off this time." She sighs but smiles. "Thank you both so much for your help in her recapture. Maybe this time we'll have better luck with her." Doubtful. She waves to us then turns and walks away and follows her staff and the van back to the hospital.

"So, shall we head home now as well?" Sheamus says to me. It isn't until that moment I realize just how tired I actually feel. Sheamus must feel the same way.

"Yea, let's go," I say as we start our walk home.

CHAPTER 16

I
t is a brisk night out but the chilled air isn't what is making me cold. Battling against someone who can use the cold and ice against you always sends chills up my spine, in more ways than one. Sheamus and I are walking down the hill from the museum in silence, neither one of us want to ruin the peace that has been created. But I know eventually it has to be talked about.

"Do you ever wonder what sets her off?" he asks me when we are at the bottom of the hill.

"Not really," which is half the truth. Before when she first started making trouble I wondered all the time what it was that set her off, whether I could do anything to help her. Now I don't even think about her. She is beyond my help. I'll leave her to the professionals. Sheamus and I just deliver her to them when we have to.

"I know you are lying," he smiles at me. "Yes, she's becomes an annoyance more times than I can count and yes she does have a warped sense of reality with you, but I know you. If you could solve her you would do it in an instant." He has me there. If I could solve Freeza's mental instability I would.

"But not for the reasons you think," I say.

"Oh trust me I wouldn't do it for her sake, either. I would do it for everyone else. She's done more than enough damage to everyone around." With that we walk some more in silence. But still his question plagues me.

"What do you think is the reason she goes off the deep end?" I ask Sheamus. He is the smart one between the two of us.

"It has to be something that happened in her childhood, it always is. Abuse, maybe she moved and lost friends and it damaged her, maybe she got yelled at one time too many, or maybe she didn't get yelled at enough. Who knows what it could be? If I knew I would say something. All I have are guesses. What do you think it is?"

"Before, I never could make connections. Now, there are just way too many times she gets set off that I think she was born with some sort of mental illness that can't be solved with therapy or just talking about her feelings." I feel slightly bad about saying she is a problem that can't be solved but sometimes that happens in the world. Some problems just can't be solved no matter how hard you try.

"So what do we do for the future?" he asks.

"We keep doing what we have to do against her. When she becomes a problem we get her to Dr. Freeview. Nothing more we can do." There honestly isn't any more we could do. She isn't like the gang problems or rogue criminals we encounter. She doesn't listen to reason, she can't be handled. There is a reason why she wanted that painting but she isn't going to tell us and it probably has no connection to anything important. We can't solve a problem unless we know why it is a problem in the first place.

"I wonder why she has such an obsession with you."

"Well that one is easy." It is true, even I know why she always is 'in love' with me even though I oppose her all the time.

"Really?" he asks quite surprised.

"I mean I was the first one that probably ever turned her down and put up a fight to her. She probably likes the power I represent or whatever it is that I did two years ago by standing up to her."

"So she likes that she can't control you," he hums interestingly. "How fascinating."

While it is interesting to be able to try and figure out why someone does something I don't care for it for Freeza. It's true and I don't mind saying it at all, I don't like her. I would go so far as to say I loathe her presence. I hate having to clean up her messes and problems that she creates every couple of months or so when she goes off the deep end. I hate how her warped sense of reality makes it seem like we are in a relationship and that the past two years never happened at all to her. She is annoying and I wish she never came here at all. I have enough to deal with that doesn't include her insane rantings.

"Penny for your thoughts?" Sheamus asks me. I realize that I have been thinking intently.

"Annoyingly ranting about Freeza in my head." I respond.

"Well you should stop. The mission is done with. Tomorrow we'll go see Scotty and tell him all is over with. With Freeza locked up in Freeview she won't be bothering us for a while. Even when she eventually leaves she won't bother us close to that extent. We have a few months Freeza free." That makes me feel better. Sheamus is right, I dwell on her too often afterwards. I have done my part and she is now someone else's problem, I just wish it didn't have to be like that. I look around and notice that we are almost home.

Soon enough we walk through our apartment door and we both realize we are quite exhausted from the events of the night.

"Well, you deserve a good night's rest. Have a good night Devon," Sheamus tells me as he heads to his room.

"Sheamus?" I call out to him before he goes into his bedroom. He looks towards me with a questioning look. "Thanks for the save tonight, you sure do have a knack for that."

He smiles back at me. "Anything for you buddy." With that he goes into his bedroom and I go into mine ready to hopefully relax the next day.

CHAPTER 17

The next morning feels as normal as it can be. I wake up at a reasonable hour, eat breakfast, and get changed all before ten. It is feeling like a real productive morning and I know it can't work out all that well in my favor.

"So, ready to go see Scotty and tell him all his problems are over?" Sheamus asks me as he walks into the living room a bit before ten. Our plan is to go to the museum and see Scotty to tell him our work was completed and Freeza has been captured and sent back to Freeview.

"I've been waiting for this the past two days. I'm more ready than ever." I get up from the couch I am sitting on but before I can take a step there is a knock on our door. Sheamus walks to the door and opens it to see a young man standing there. He keeps putting his hands through his hair and for some reason I recognize him. Then it hits me. "You're the guy from the lobby at Freeview. The nervous looking one that couldn't stop staring at the commotion happening." The guy looks startled that I recognize him.

"Oh, yea you are. What are you doing here?" Sheamus responds to my recognition.

"Well I have a message from Dr. Freeview. She would like Devon to come down to her office right away. It's urgent," the man says nervously. Why is he always so nervous? It's not like we're going to hurt him.

"Thank you I'll be right there." I say nodding to the guy and he turns to leave while Sheamus shuts the door.

"So new plan, I'll go update Scotty and you are going to Freeview to see what it is she needs." Sheamus tells me.

"You sure you aren't interested in what Freeview wants me for?"

He shakes his head "She specifically named you to come so obviously it would be best if you just showed up alone." Makes sense.

"Ok, well you might as well just come back here and wait for me since I don't know how long this will take." He nods and then proceeds to leave the apartment with me right behind him.

Outside we go our separate ways with me heading towards the Freeview Hospital and him heading towards the museum. I am interested to know what Freeview has to talk to me about. If somehow Freeza escaped we would have been told immediately and gone out to look for her, so she hasn't escaped.

Another possibility is that for some reason Dr. Freeview has to release Freeza earlier than any of us expected. Maybe even her treatment is completed and she wants to warn us ahead of time. That would make our lives a lot more difficult in the coming weeks.

But a third possibility was available. One that was better than the other two. Dr. Freeview may have made a breakthrough with Freeza's treatment and made progress in lessening her mental outbursts. It is very unlikely but I can only hope.

I arrive at the hospital quite quickly since I am curious to see what it is I am being brought out here for. I walk into the lobby and wave to the girl who is on duty at the receptionist desk and head towards Dr. Freeview's office. When I arrive I knock on the door and am startled when she looks at me and jumps up to greet me.

"Devon I am glad you are here. Quick, come with me." She starts dragging me down the hallway away from her office. "You'll never believe it, I've had a major breakthrough with Freeza's treatment. I wasn't even expecting it but it's happened and I wanted you down here to experience it with me and maybe give me insight into what might be going on here." She is talking quite quickly and I can't even get a word in. We stop outside a door and she turns to me but I still have some questions for the doctor.

"Hold on, what are you talking about?"

"I was able to break through the barrier that she held up against me."

"You are kidding me." The barrier she is talking about was a mental barrier that Freeza had created early on in her therapy sessions with Dr. Freeview who tried to get into her memories to try and understand her more. I never understand how Freeza does it and it is a constant problem for Dr. Freeview to overcome. It sounds like she did it.

"No I am not and I want you to come along on the journey with me."

"You mean you can do that?" I ask perplexed.

"Yes, now come on, she's sedated and I don't know how long we have." She opens the door in front of us and shoves me inside.

I am greeted by a hospital room environment. It is a small room with a hospital bed. On the bed is Freeza just lying there in a hospital gown and what looks like a couple of IVs attached to her arms. I tense up seeing her but Dr. Freeview puts her hand on my shoulder.

"I told you, she's sedated now so she doesn't even know we are in here." She moves closer to the bed and motions me over. When I join her she grabs my hand and puts her other hand onto Freeza's head. "Are you ready for this? It will be a bit shocking when it happens but you'll be ok."

"I guess I am ready," I say apprehensively. I am not sure what to expect but she doesn't seem to pick up on my nervousness. Without warning I start noticing the colors of the walls melting away and even the walls themselves melt along with them. Everything around us seems to be changing until I realize we are outside in an unfamiliar location, no longer in Prison City. I am not sure where we are.

"Devon," Dr. Freeview looks at me, "welcome to Freeza's memory."

CHAPTER 18

Freeza's memory. We are in Freeza's memory. I can't explain it but it has to be the correct explanation of why we are in a different location. I wonder where we are inside of it. Or at least when we are in Freeza's life. She has to be here somewhere. It is her memory after all.

"Considering Freeza is quite quiet about her life before Prison City I have no idea when we are in her timeline," Dr. Freeview says to me.

Looking around, I see that we are on the sidewalk of a busy street. I can see houses all around us that are basically on top of one another and people are walking all around us. I am not sure how they don't notice we are right there until someone literally walks through me. I am flabbergasted at what just happened and turn to Dr. Freeview for answers. The look she gives me is just unamused.

"You do realize we didn't time travel right? We aren't really here. Your physical body is still at the hospital right now in a sort of sleep state. Your subconscious is here right now. You don't exist in this world but your mind has given you a body for this exact purpose of moving around." I look down and realize that she is correct. I have two arms, a body, and two legs. I guess my mind knows what it is doing better than I do. "Now come on we don't have much time. There's Freeza." She points a distance away and there is Freeza, looking a bit younger than is now, but looking just as paranoid as ever. She is knocking into people but not really understanding what she is doing, since they would give her ugly looks but she doesn't even look away from in front of her. It is quite strange. Almost like she is in a trance but has to keep moving forward. She moves right past us without so much as giving us a look. Thank you for not actually being here. But before I can say another word Dr. Freeview grabs my arm and starts pulling me along right behind Freeza.

"You know I can follow you without you dragging me along right?" I ask her. She looks down and releases my arm almost like she didn't even know that she was doing it.

"Sorry, I just don't want to lose her."

"Trust me I don't want to either. But where exactly are we?"

"I'm not sure, but I think we'll find out in a just a few minutes. I feel she will bring us to the answers of the questions we are asking."

We continue walking right behind Freeza who every so often will look around almost like she is expecting to be followed or confronted. Soon enough she stops in front of what looks like an apartment building. It is a brick building that looks like it is ten stories tall and seems to have been here for a long time. She looks around her and then a police car comes zooming past us. She looks like she is going to have a heart attack and quickly rushes into the building.

I've seen that look before, I've had that look before. I know exactly where we are, when we are and what is going on.

Freeza quickly gets into an elevator and we follow her in, she presses a button for the fifth floor and the doors close and the elevator starts moving upwards.

"I know what's going on," I say to Dr. Freeview who looks at me in astonishment. "Roughly I would say we are in two years ago. We are in Grand Meadow City. This is the point where Freeza gets arrested and is sent to Prison City."

"But how would you know this? I know where she is from and only rough details of her arrest," she asks me. I look up and see we are only one floor away from the fifth floor, the floor where Freeza's life will change forever.

"It helps that Sheamus and I have special access to prisoners' files due to our job. But trust me I know what is going to happen." Dr. Freeview just looks at me curiously but doesn't say anything more since the bell for the floor dings and the doors open. Freeza walks out and turns to the left and starts walking down the hallway. We follow right behind her. She stops at a door, numbered 505, and knocks on it. In less than ten seconds the door opens up and a girl of about my age is standing there. She is roughly Freeza's height but has long, blond hair and is dressed quite nicely for just being in an apartment.

"Adelina? What are you doing here?" the woman says to Freeza.

"Morgan, is it ok if I come in?" Freeza asks. The woman looks puzzled for a few seconds but steps aside so Freeza can go inside. We also walk into the apartment.

It looks nicely furnished and probably had an expert designer brought in to make it look even better. From the small entryway Freeza is brought into what is probably the living room and sits down on the couch that is there. It is a bright gold colored three person couch and looks like the rest of the room: expensive.

"Adelina I haven't seen you in months, what are you doing here?" Morgan asks.

"I am in trouble. I need your help." I turn to Dr. Freeview and decide it was time to spill the truth.

"Since it's all going to come out here and now I better prepare you for what's about to come in the next oh say twenty to thirty minutes."

"What's about to come?" She says raising an eyebrow at me. I take a deep breath and go for the plunge.

"By the age of eight she had been showing signs of mental problems but her parents kept them hidden so as to not show shame on the family. By the age of sixteen people started questioning how mentally healthy she was and what was going on with the family. The family at that point decided to try using a private therapist but it was too late. Her mental outbursts were becoming more frequent and become more and more irrational. When she was eighteen her parents decided to keep her out of the public eye and a year later they seriously considered having her mentally institutionalized. Two months before this she grew tired of trying to keep her parents happy and the rich lifestyle was putting unnecessary pressure on her to be normal when she was far from it. So she decided to run away. Before all that she went by the name of Adelina Lupo. She took the name Freeza to distance herself from the lifestyle. For two months she kept away from everyone she knew and resorted to stealing to obtain what she needed. Today, she robbed a convenience store but the person on duty called the cops quickly and, recognizing her, sent them out to search for her which they are doing now," I say as I explain the past of Freeza.

"How do you know all this?" Dr. Freeview asks me raising an eyebrow almost like she doesn't believe me.

"I told you I have access to special files. Of course they are only the arrest records of what puts prisoners in the city in the first place but still it helps. Also they both just talked about exactly what I just told you." I point at the two women on the couch.

"I'm not lying I just robbed a store and I am pretty sure the cops are after me. I won't be locked away. Please you need to hide me away," Freeza speaks quite desperately. If we didn't know who she is it would sound sad but Dr. Freeview and I aren't moved.

"Get ready for the worst decision Morgan Cramer could make," I say. Before Dr. Freeview can say another word Morgan stands up.

"Here I think you need some water. Just sit tight and I'll be back in a second." She strolls out of the room into what I think is the connecting kitchen. I follow right behind her but Dr. Freeview wants to stick with Freeza and I don't allow that.

"Trust me you'll want to be in here."

"Why?" she asks but I don't respond and only point at Morgan who withdraws her cell phone from her pocket and starts typing on it. Dr. Freeview peeks over her shoulder and reads back what is being written.

"Mom, I really hope you get this because I need you to call the police. Adelina is at my apartment now. She just confessed to me that she robbed a convenience store and she seemed very unstable. Please send the police over to my apartment right away. I don't feel safe." She looks right at me with fear in her eyes.

"Her mistake."

CHAPTER 19

Morgan puts her phone away, breathes a sigh of relief, goes into the fridge and grabs two bottles of water and leaves the kitchen. Dr. Freeview gives me a look like something in between pleading and begging. She knows where this is going. But she could never understand just how bad the situation will truly get.

"What happens?" she asks. Two words that are just so upsetting.

"You will see in five minutes." I walk out of the kitchen to see the women sitting down on the couch talking to each other. Freeza looks extremely calm and almost joyful at having her friend stick up for her, if only she knew. Well she would soon.

"Who is Morgan to Freeza?" Dr. Freeview asks.

"Best friends," I answer. I decide to listen to their conversation and see what is happening.

"So Adelina, where have you been living anyway?" Morgan asks.

"Please Morgan call me Freeza. It's what I go by now, gives me a sense of freedom from my old life," Morgan nods and Freeza continues. "I've been pretty much living wherever I am. If I find an abandoned building I'll sleep there. Maybe some days I'll sleep in the forest. It really doesn't matter to me." Morgan once again nods and seems to look slightly uncomfortable, she pulls out her phone and sighs. It was probably her mother responding that the police are going to show up.

The two women keep chatting some more until Freeza decides to get up and walk around, looking around the room. "You certainly have a nice apartment. I'm sorry I never was able to come and see it. My parents had forbidden me to leave the house since they didn't want me to ruin their image."

"It's ok I understand. Sometimes your parents can be quite difficult." While Freeza is walking around Morgan once again looks at her phone.

"How much time has passed?" Dr. Freeview asks me.

"I think about ten minutes. If they are serious about Freeza they should be here any minute now." Freeza walks over to a window and looks out and makes a gasping noise. She slowly turns around to face Morgan who, noticing her reaction quickly gets to her feet.

"What's wrong?" Morgan asks. The look on her face basically gives away that she knows what is up and if it wasn't so terrifying it would be funny.

"There are police cars outside. Four to be precise. They shouldn't even have any clue I am here. They couldn't know I was here, so how the hell do they know I am here? Morgan, do you have any idea of how they know I am here?" Freeza slowly takes a step towards Morgan with each sentence until she is face to face with the woman. Morgan stands her ground but looks like she wants to run away as fast as possible.

"I called them Adelina. You aren't ok. You've committed crimes and potentially could hurt someone. I can't hide you from them. You need to go with the police." She almost sounds like she is pleading but more tries to stay as firm and strong as possible. Then there is a loud banging on the apartment door.

"Adelina Lupo, we know you are in there! Come out with your hands up!" Freeza looks startled and quickly uses a cold blast from her hands and produces ice all over the apartment door, effectively freezing it shut. Suddenly Morgan screams and starts running into the back part of the apartment but Freeza sends another cold blast at her, freezing her feet to the ground.

"Adelina, no! You can't do this. Please don't do this!" Morgan yells. She looks like she is not only afraid of Freeza but she also regrets every decision she has made up to this point.

"Now why not? Why should I let you go after you betrayed me? You are supposed to be my friend, my best friend and you ruined that by calling the police. Do you know what they are going to do? They are going to institutionalize me and I will be stuck there for the rest of my life. My parents end up winning and I lose. That is what you did to me. You think I am insane. You think I'm a bad person. Well I think you're the crazy one for making me your enemy." Morgan is bawling her eyes out at this point and only being held upright because of the ice that has encased her feet and legs. Freeza is ranting and raving about like a lunatic.

Dr. Freeview and I are just standing around looking unhappy about the whole situation. Dr. Freeview doesn't know how it all ends but I do. "You are so going to pay for this." Freeza at this point stands face to face with Morgan and raises one of her hands directly towards her face.

"No. Please!" Morgan pleads crying her eyes out, drawing out the please part. Dr. Freeview looks stunned but suddenly a large man in a police uniform appears right behind Freeza and hits her from behind with a club and she falls to the floor without launching an attack. Dr. Freeview, Morgan and even Freeza look stunned at the events that just transpired.

"Who the hell are you?" Freeza tries to get up but the man picks her up and holds her hands behind her back and stops her from moving.

"Where did he come from?" Dr. Freeview asks me.

"He's a police officer. He has the power of invisibility. Apparently he went invisible and climbed in through the fire escape in the bedroom before Freeza saw them approach. He's been watching the whole situation like we've been." I explain from what I know from the arrest report that was given.

"We are all clear," the man says into a radio on his shoulder. Not even ten seconds later the apartment door comes crashing down and a hoard of four police officers come storming into the apartment. Two of them cuff Freeza's hands behind her back while the other two chip away at the ice on Morgan who is still crying and looking afraid. The three officers with Freeza start pulling her away but not before she starts wailing and putting up a fuss. Morgan is pulled away towards a bedroom but not before Freeza starts screaming.

"You can't do this to me! You used to be my friend and now you are nothing to me! You'll be nothing to anyone ever again! You're done for! You hear me, done!" Freeza is bellowing at anyone who will listen to her. Soon enough the officers get her under control.

"Wait, why is it that this memory sent her over the edge this time?" I wonder out loud. It doesn't make sense. She must remember this point of her life every day while she's in Prison City so why is it that she went off the deep end for a painting? I look around the room and spot the item that connects it all. "Look." I point at it for Dr. Freeview.

"Well that is extraordinary." We both walk over to a wall that holds a painting of a field with two deer, a couple of squirrels and a lion, all either picking at the grass or just resting around. In the corner of the painting was the signature showcasing the artwork to be by Scotty Braun. It is truly amazing. We both went back to observing the commotion that is still going on in the living room.

"This is how she gets arrested, by being betrayed by her close friend. No wonder she's so screwed up. She probably loses it at the sight of a human being. This most definitely destroyed any correct mentality in her brain," Dr. Freeview tells me. But something is slightly bugging me. The air feels a bit cooler and one of the officers has a slight blue-ish tinge to him yet he isn't acting abnormally. Dr. Freeview is still talking so she isn't seeing what I am seeing.

"Ummm something isn't right. She doesn't launch any type of attack once she goes down, so why is it getting colder?" I ask Dr. Freeview who looks up and sees what I am seeing. She turns around and gasps. I turn around as well to see one of the walls starting to get covered in ice. What is going on here?

Suddenly everything starts to look faded in color and starts to slow down. Soon all the walls around us are covered in ice and everyone starts becoming ice statues. The place we are in no longer looks like an apartment but more like an ice wonderland.

"GET OUT!" a voice shouts from somewhere. Since everything is ice around us and no one is around we couldn't be sure where it is coming from.

"What was that?" We both look around but can't see anything.

Everything is clear blue and looks similar and at this point we can't tell what direction we are facing. Suddenly from in front of us the ice opens up and Freeza walks out from it, the opening closing behind her. The weird thing about the Freeza in front of us is that she is wearing the same exact clothing from the day before, plus she appears older than the version we just saw of her.

"No." Dr. Freeview says quietly from beside me.

"Get out of my memories. GET OUT OF MY HEAD!" Freeza yells.

In a blink of an eye we are gone from the ice wonderland and back in the hospital room. I am disoriented, Dr. Freeview is gasping for air, and Freeza is writhing around on her hospital bed. Before we can do anything her eyes shoot open and she leaps to her hands and knees and gives us the most unsatisfying angry look I have ever seen. She suddenly lunges at me but I am quicker by creating a shadow hand and pinning her against the wall that is across from us. Her hands are firing out cold blasts but since they are held against the wall they are harmlessly firing out from her and not towards us.

"I really think you should sedate her!" I scream since I have to be heard over Freeza's yelling.

"What do you think I'm trying to do, let her just use up all her energy? I'm trying to find the drugs!" She yells back, finally pulling out a syringe from the drawer she is searching in. "Hold her as tightly as possible." I use my shadow hand and put a bit more of a grip on her entire body and she stops struggling as much as she is. Dr. Freeview then goes over and sticks the syringe into Freeza's arm. "Ok, you're good now, you can put her back on the bed." Freeza looks at us wide-eyed.

"No you will not go back into my memories. THOSE ARE MINE! Get away from me." I easily lift her up from her position against the wall, since she is starting to slump a bit, and put her back on the bed. Even though she has only been injected within the past twenty seconds the drug's effects are already kicking in. Within a minute she is already out like a light. Dr. Freeview puts away the syringe she has and takes off the latex gloves she put on. She pulls me out of the room and we stand in the hallway outside Freeza's room.

"Well now you officially know how Freeza got here," I say solemnly. I may not like Freeza but I do understand what it means to be betrayed.

"Yes I do," she says just as downhearted.

"Now I have a question for you."

"Ok," she says straightening herself up a bit.

"What the hell happened in her memories? How was she able to change them up and force us out like that?" I ask. It is extremely puzzling to me to have it all happen.

"You saw her at the museum. She was over the edge of a mental breakdown and suddenly she was able to basically produce a blizzard from her mouth."

"Yes, I coined that as her blizzard breath." I am quite amused at coming up with such an original name. But Dr. Freeview looks unimpressed.

"Whatever it is called she wasn't able to do it before and suddenly she can do it. While she never allowed me into her memories before today I certainly can say that her psychosis more than likely is what gave her the ability to overcome my power on her. You may think it's all annoying but her psychosis can be pretty extraordinary in times of need for her." It is actually pretty amazing to think she can advance her own powers and be able to negate someone else's powers. She still bugs me though.

"How long have we been gone for?" It feels like we have been gone for upwards of an hour.

She looks up at a clock on the wall before answering. "Probably close to ten minutes." The surprise on my face must have been obvious since she quickly adds in that time moves faster in memories. Makes sense.

We just stay silent for a couple of minutes before Dr. Freeview speaks again. "To think that somehow she was able to go through this memory and look at that painting and reread the signature on the painting and then connect it to the same painter that was in here with her."

"At least we know what made her lose it this time around," I say. Thankfully, since sometimes we never can figure it out. We stand around a bit longer until I realize it is time for me to go.

"You've unlocked her mysterious past, so it's time for me to get going. Thanks though for inviting me to this."

"No problem. See you around." With that I leave her as she walks back into Freeza's room.

I am glad this mission is over. No more insanity for me for a long while hopefully.

CHAPTER 20

The walk back home allows me to decompress and relax from the eventful three days I've had. It's not until you actually get away from an eventful time that you realize you have had an eventful time. Soon enough I am walking into my apartment seeing Sheamus come out of the kitchen with a bowl of spaghetti.

"Glad you are back. How did it go?" he asks me as he sits on the couch. I join right next to him.

"Pretty strange and unexpected. You go first though. How was Scotty with the news of Freeza's capture?"

"He took it wonderfully. Actually he remembered that Freeza came into the museum about a week ago. He recognized her from, well, from her notoriety in Prison City but didn't think any harm would come from her being in his museum. If anything he was happy to have a potential new customer. He realized she was quite enthralled with The Frozen Abyss but didn't think it was weird at the time." While I am listening to him something clicks in my brain about everything.

"The notes." Sheamus raises an eyebrow at me, showcasing his confusion. "I understand how the notes connect to her now." Once again he still isn't connecting it at all. He puts down his bowl of pasta and just stares at me. "She works for the Prison City Magazine. She has access to different issues of the magazine. She probably cut out the different letters from those issues for the notes." Sheamus makes a long oh sound and facepalms.

"Damn I'm such an idiot. I didn't even think of that. She's never used notes before so I never put her occupation and them together. Good catch on that one." He goes back to his bowl of spaghetti. "Now it's your turn. How was your meeting with Dr. Freeview?"

"It was enlightening. She was able to break through the barrier Freeza produced and could access her memories. Well at least one of her memories. She allowed me to join in on the viewing." Sheamus looks up at that information and smiles, looking kind of excited at the news.

"Well what memory did she unlock?"

"When she got arrested. We landed at the point when she was heading to Morgan's apartment. We followed straight to the apartment and saw her go inside. Once inside we saw the moment that Morgan texted her mother to call the police on Freeza. Then we saw the whole hostage situation. Finally we saw her captured from the officer with the invisibility powers. All in all it was exciting to actually see it happen instead of reading about it." Sheamus nods looking quite pleased at my mini adventure for the day. "Oh I almost forgot to mention that I figured out why Freeza lost it this time around." Sheamus looks excited at what I am about to produce for it. It is always good to be able to figure out the motive. "Morgan had a painting that was made and signed by Scotty Braun." Sheamus looks amazed when I tell him that.

"That's incredible! To think she could remember the signature on a painting and then connect it to someone in here with her. That explains so much about her actions the past couple of days." Of course that's all it explains. It only helps us with her actions this time around. It more than likely will only help for this time.

"Anything else happen after it all?" he asks.

"Yea the most interesting part. Somehow she was able to break free of Dr. Freeview's power and force us out of her memories." Sheamus looks at me amazed and stunned.

"How did she do that?"

"I'm not sure how she was able to do it but suddenly the room we were in was filled with ice and she just appeared out of nowhere. She screamed at us to get out of her memories and in a blink we were back in her hospital room. She then tried to attack us but luckily, with some help from me, Dr. Freeview was able to sedate her. It was all really a trying time." Sheamus still looks amazed at everything I went through and puts down his bowl again and leans back against the couch. I'm not sure what he is thinking about until a smile comes on his face and I slowly figure it out.

"Of all the psychos in that hospital that we have to deal with, our most common threat is the girl that has an undeniable crush on you." He looks at me and just bursts out laughing. Yes it is my luck that I have the attention of a woman who wants to love me, kill me, and ruin my life all in the same second. She may have a dangerous power but the reason I try to avoid her at all costs is that she is absolutely draining on my energy. She makes me want to never want to interact with a non-normal person again.

"Why is it that she loves me but hates you with a burning passion? Pun not intended."

"Well it's either you're undeniable charm or dangerous lifestyle. But I personally think she's just jealous that you spend so much time with me." He smirks at me trying to defuse the slight annoyance I have on my face that always comes up when I talk about Freeza.

"Can I talk about something serious?" He stops smiling and sits up forward and nods, I have his full attention. "I don't hate her because of the psychosis. I don't hate her because of her personality really." He looks at me interested probably wondering where all this is coming from. "I hate what she does because of her psychosis. I hate that she can be so disruptive because of a mental illness. I may not be able to understand what goes on in her head during one of her episodes but I certainly can see the destruction that she causes around her. The destruction that I usually have to make right. I feel like I'm her parental guardian and I don't want to be. I want her to understand she has a problem and take steps to keep her illness under control." I let all my feelings on the situation out, some of which Sheamus already knows and understands.

"It can be difficult and you know just as well as I do that this job not only is dangerous but thankless and can get on every last one of your nerves at the same time." It is extremely true. There is only one reason why we do all this. "We do it to make up for what we did to end up in this awful place. We do it because it's the right thing to do. We do it to maybe help out one other person from destroying their own life and showing them a different way of doing things."

"You know you are right. Why are you always right?"

He is smiling at me while going back to his bowl of pasta "Because someone has to counteract all the wrong things you say" It gets strangely silent between us while Sheamus is looking into his bowl. "Freeza is still the psychoess of Prison City?" he asks. I chuckle. He would know how to go from serious to making a joke in less than thirty seconds.

"She is the craziest person in Prison City." With that we laugh knowing that beyond our apartment things can be rough and tough but we still have to carry on and do what we want and need to do to make things right for our past. But it can be nice being able to have a safe little space in our apartment to just joke around and have fun together without being worried about anything else for a while.

ABOUT THE AUTHOR

Jamie Farrell was born in Massachusetts and has lived there his whole life. He graduated from college with a degree in criminal justice and is also an Eagle Scout. He's a big fan of sci-fi, fantasy, and adventure. He is a huge fan of animals and lives with two dogs and also enjoys reading.